Rise of the Demigods

KATIE CROSS

KCW

To Kaley, a stellar human.
To Kaley, my shining star in the dark.
To Kaley, the ultimate Canadian beta reader.

Chapter One

The thud of my feet slapping the floor shot through my body until I felt it in my jaw.

The heavy steps zipped all the way to the back of my head, where my scalp prickled. Despite the discomfort, I paced back and forth across Scarlett's office anyway.

If I stopped moving, the news Scarlett had just delivered would spiral through my mind over and over again. If I stopped moving, the ramifications would be all-too-real.

Across from me, Scarlett continued, oblivious to my internal distress.

"I'm sorry, Bianca," she murmured, "but a five minute time slot in which you can speak to the Council is, frankly, better than I expected. It's not an outright rejection."

I stopped to glare at her.

She glowered back.

My nostrils flared as I resumed my pacing, submitting to her glacial authority. Of *course* the Council gave me five minutes. Five minutes would barely give me room for ten sentences. Nothing could be decided.

That was, perhaps, their goal.

Thud. Thud. Thud. Spin.
Thud. Thud. Thud. Spin.

Scarlett's voice became background noise now, but my mind tracked it. "Some of the Council made allusions to the possibility that they would discuss allowing women into the Guardians and . . . all that would mean. But it's not a priority right now."

Her reply stopped me in my tracks yet again. They would *talk* about letting women into the Guardians?

"That's it?" I cried.

She held up a hand. "Progress moves at the speed of politics. You cannot expect the Network to have the funds and ability to institute a Sisterhood of Protectors when they don't even allow women into the Guardians. We have to take this in steps."

"At this rate I'll be too old to be in the Sisterhood, if it even happens at all."

"Don't be dramatic."

"I'm afraid that I'm not."

"It's the best we can do while demigods are on the loose in Alkarra, Bianca. You must admit, even a small chance to speak with them is progress."

Thud. Thud. Thud. Spin.
Thud. Thud. Th—

"In the name of the good gods," she snapped. "Stop. Pacing."

My right foot hovered an inch off the floor, then slowly lowered. I turned to face her and let out a long breath.

"Right. Sorry."

Scarlett eyed me, then shook her head.

"You're too wound up. We won't decide anything with you acting so frantically. Council support for the Sisterhood will only come with strategy and patience, not destroying my floorboards."

She had a point—my patience could use a lot of work. If the topic of lacking support for a Sisterhood wasn't naturally anxiety-inducing enough, then the time that had passed since the end of the Celebration *was.*

Two months ago, the Celebration of peace that all four Networks participated in had fallen to shreds. Igor, High Priest of the South, revealed himself as a demigod named Bram. He'd come to Alkarra from Alaysia, the land of the gods, to draw power and prestige amongst other demigods.

His plan involved forcing Southern Network witches— magicless after the Network War over three years ago— into allegiance with him. Such allegiance would give Southern Network witches limited access to god magic, but they had to serve him until they died.

Fortunately, due to a combination of luck, risk, and hope, a mortal girl named Ava and I had found Bram and outed him. After his attempted power-grab had been prevented, Baxter returned Bram to Alaysia, where Bram would be punished in a *manner befitting the gods.*

Except . . . Bram's exit from Alkarra didn't sit well with many of us. Would the discipline even happen? Who was in charge of Bram's punishment?

What if he escaped?

How would we ever know?

I shook off my concerns regarding Bram. I couldn't focus on that now. When Bram left, he'd adamantly declared that other demigods were already here, ready to turn witches to mortals and take their allegiance.

Except . . . no other demigods had been caught in the months that had passed.

With a sigh, I threw myself into a padded chair near the fire. Flames crackled in the rectangular, stone hearth, which stood as tall as me. Light flickered into the darkening room. A gust of wind shivered the windows on either side of the fire and I thought I saw a star pop out of the night sky.

My thoughts skimmed over Letum Wood and the distant keen of the trees outside. Their voices murmured, low in my thoughts, but I turned back to the topic at hand.

Sisterhood.

Stalled progress.

Lack of Council support.

My knee hopped around in a wild bounce as my thoughts built.

Most of the Council's focus since the end of the Celebration had turned to managing inner Network affairs while Papa focused on the other Networks. The general panic amongst our witches meant the Council's attention was understandably placed on cleaning up the mess that the Celebration left behind. Soon, though, it would *need* to shift to public safety.

The demigods that lingered in Alkarra would be caught, even though they hadn't been found yet, and we needed to be ready.

"The Council won't respond well to me putting the idea of a Sisterhood forward," Scarlett said, stating something we already knew. I imagined she had a mental checklist of sorts. She always verbally ran through a list of things we strongly presumed before we could advance to action items. "I need to maintain my current position of trust amongst the Council and the Sisterhood will not inspire it."

"You need to stay distant from the Sisterhood," I murmured in agreement.

In other words: the Sisterhood was mine to live or die with. Any success or failure belonged solely with me. Scarlett would be a vague figure in the background that no one else knew about, but would offer advice privately to me as needed. When it made sense to do so, the Sisterhood would receive Scarlett's full endorsement and assistance.

"We've already ruled out that funding isn't an issue because we could use the training equipment that the Brotherhood uses," I pointed out, "which will help. I'm happy to volunteer my time until we have a significant plan for currency."

Scarlett's sharp gaze didn't frighten me. She didn't like that I wouldn't be compensated for my work at first, but with Papa as High Priest and my own cottage in Letum Wood where the trees kept me safe, I could lose payment without fear of starvation for a little while.

For the Sisterhood, it would be worth it.

"For now," she added.

I waved that off.

Calm had returned to her general mien, which helped me relax. I returned to my feet, but didn't pace.

"What if we can pull Matthias to our cause?" I asked as the idea popped into my head.

The Head of Protectors was a daunting man. The Council had approved Matthias when Papa instituted him. Not that their contrary opinions would have stopped Papa, but it helped keep the waters smooth.

As Highest Witch, he controlled Network relationships, the Brotherhood of Protectors, and the Guardians. The Council of ten other witches worked within the Network and helped with everything else the witches needed.

Scarlett's brow grew heavy in thought, so I pushed into the fresh idea.

"If Matthias publicly supported the founding of the Sisterhood, then you could too. You wouldn't be in jeopardy of harming your trusted relationship with the Council because there would be two high-ranking leaders behind it. That would give us a greater ability to find other female candidates and start the discussion on how the Brotherhood and Sisterhood could interact."

"What about the matter of females not being allowed into the Guardians?"

"Different issue, if you ask me."

She made a noise in her throat. "I disagree, but a point could be made."

I stopped, faced her, and threw my hands in the air. "I can't believe we didn't think of this before! It's a win-win. Matthias is the answer!"

Her expression gave nothing away as she studied me. "Why do you think he's critical?" she asked. Her crisp tone suggested she already knew what I'd say, but wanted to hear it from my lips.

"Because he's the face of the Brotherhood, just as I will be for the Sisterhood. If the two of us worked together, the Council wouldn't say no. They're terrified of him," I added under my breath, "just like they're scared of the rest of the Brotherhood."

A flicker of annoyance registered on her face.

"The Council isn't *scared* of him, Bianca, and they wouldn't think highly of your suggestion. They know where to place their respect. There's a difference and it's significant. Regardless . . ." She trailed away, which gave me my first moment of hope. "You may be onto something."

Scarlett lapsed into silence. The firelight cut a sharp angle against her jaw, sending glimmering light onto her dark hair. A crimson dress covered her arms all the way to her wrists, sliding to the floor with a quiet whisper of silk skirts. Flat, black buttons edged up the side of the bodice, beneath her arm. Even with her stern, thoughtful expression, Scarlett had an old-world loveliness about her.

A cold draft slipped through the room. I sent a quick incantation to the fireplace to bolster the fire. Flames bounced to life. Firewood arranged itself in the coals from a pile near the window.

With satisfaction, I watched the magic play out. How good it felt. After losing my ability to do magic for weeks, I still relished in the opportunity to do it now, months after it had been restored.

Scarlett's voice broke through my thoughts.

"I don't know, Bianca. I can't imagine Matthias will be any more excited about the Sisterhood than the Council."

If Scarlett had accepted any idea I presented without suspicion, I would have been concerned. Her skepticism was a reassuring path, though fraught with peril.

"Let me talk to Matthias. It's our best avenue. And easiest," I tacked on. "Imagine how quick this process will be with him on board. Plus, I won't mention you at all. I'll just take myself into it."

Scarlett's eyes tapered to slits. Clearly, I hadn't won her over. Soon enough, I would. Matthias had always had a sort of affection for me. As much as he did for any other witch, which wasn't a lot. He'd never been a *soft* kind of man.

"What would you say to him?"

"I would tell him that we need a firm plan to deal with the demigod problem, and that it has to be surprising and different. The demigods use thought magic, which makes their magic faster, more versatile, and for some, maybe more powerful than our everyday magic. Which means it's time for outside help."

She scowled.

"You're going to tell the Head of Protectors that *he* needs help? From a child?"

I bristled. "I'm not a child, thank you. I'm twenty-two years old. I believe surviving a kidnapping and fighting a war has proven that."

She sighed and managed to sound a little contrite. "A woman, forgive me. Impatience aside, you have come a long way since you were a young girl who presented herself late to

Miss Mabel's School for Girls. Regardless, no Protector, particularly not Matthias, is going to take such a suggestion well."

"Agreed. So I'll say something else." I shrugged. "I don't know, I'll figure it out when I get there."

Scarlett rolled her eyes. "We're all doomed, then."

"This can work!"

"Not if you're going to tell him that he can't handle this threat without you. Bianca, be reasonable."

I looked away, silent in my own frustration. Scarlett and I had always butted heads. Our attempt to work together on the Sisterhood had only made it worse.

"Let's not decide tonight," I said. "Tomorrow is soon enough. Then we can sleep on it, and I'll think it over."

Scarlett pushed away from her desk, strode to the window, and peered outside. A flurry of snow fell over the top of Letum Wood in a gentle, drifting pattern. Spots of sky remained open in the distance, uncluttered by the latticed shower. Her reflection in the tall panes of glass appeared troubled.

"How is your magic?" she asked.

I flexed my clenched fingers and sat back down.

"Fine."

"Is that true?"

"Of course it's true. It's fine."

Unpredictable and strange, I thought to add, but decided not to.

Goddess magic buzzed inside me, the way it always used to. The feeling ran deep, like it made my bones sing. Its return hadn't been what I expected. I'd imagined it to be a seamless transition, right back to the witch I had been before. It wasn't. Compared to the utter silence of my body when I had no magic in it, the magic felt . . . busy. Not restless, but crowded.

Maybe even angry.

The sea goddess, Prana, had restored the magic I'd lost when I met Ava, but my gratitude for her gesture straddled a wary line. Prana didn't strike me as a goddess to meddle with. She had been my only available option if I wanted my magic back, at least at that moment, so I took the opportunity.

Unfortunately, the fickle goddess magic wasn't inclined to obey me in the same way.

At random moments, heat would flare in my body, like the god magic had never left. I'd go days without feeling god magic, then it would return with painless fire and swift vengeance. In those moments, the goddess magic became unpredictable. Irregular. Like I had two opposing forces in my body.

My gaze darted to the clock. "I need to go. Thanks for meeting with me. I'll speak with Matthias this week and then let you know, all right?" I forced cheer back into my voice. "Once we recruit him into our plan, this will be easy!"

Her expression clouded.

"I urge you to be cautious, Bianca. Matthias will see you as competition, not support. He would desire neither. Any approach to Matthias should be done carefully."

"Sure. This will be just fine."

"The Sisterhood is yours," she murmured in a voice that clearly absolved her of responsibility.

My bright smile didn't assuage her worry, but she nodded once nonetheless. A tap came on her door, and one of her Assistants peered through the crack.

"Your 4:00 appointment, High Priestess."

"Thank you," Scarlett called. "Bianca was just leaving."

Taking that as my dismissal, I transported away.

* * *

Chatham City bustled like hens in a pen.

Witches moved here and there in various forms of disarray. A magic-driven cart filled with quacking ducks slipped past in a flurry of feathers and agitated sounds. Scrolls sealed with wax zipped overhead to be delivered to witches on the other side of the city. Smoke and ash and a hint of refuse lingered in the air, hovering over the dirt-caked cobblestone road.

Letum Wood swamped the city in the background, like a wall on two sides. I navigated the busy rush of witches as they headed along Chatham road, toward the castle. Kids scampered, laughing, as silk banners trailed behind their grubby hands.

Normally, I'd issue an invisibility incantation and walk around the edges to avoid being seen. Crowds agitated my god magic in an unpredictable way. I could be in a crush of people and not feel the heat at all, while other times it warmed to life on quiet roads. Never painful, but always present.

Any situation that robbed the predictability of my goddess magic made me uneasy, like walking on eggshells in my own mind.

A chilly day broke overhead as I made my way through the crowd, a hood pulled over my black hair. My eyes were my biggest giveaway. Gray as slate, sometimes a hint of blue. Most witches confirmed my identity with my eyes.

Mama's eyes.

The thought of her gave me a little courage. I pulled the cloak tighter around my shoulders and pressed into the blustery day. Snow spit out in lazy, random intervals. Thankfully, Sanako, my friend from the Western Network and a Librarian at the Great Library of Burke, had sold me a new pair of long boots her father made.

"Durable," she'd said. "The cord won't ever break. My baba found a grimoire on strengthening spells that worked on the straps."

The boots were leather and fur-lined. They extended all

the way to my knees. Despite the slushy road, a spell repelled the moisture and left my toes toasty warm. Now, they carried me away from the castle and deeper into the city. After winding through closely-built alleys, past newsscroll hawkers and Miss Holly's Candy store, I stopped in front of a bright, bustling, three-story building on a corner.

Piccadilly Pub.

The sharp tang of ipsum emanated from inside, floating alongside the smell of fresh pretzel bread. Above the pub, several stories of windows and brick lingered.

I glanced up at one set of windows in particular. Against the gloomy sky, I thought I saw the gentle glow of a candle.

With a sigh, I lifted a foot to go inside, then stopped. A cart darted in front of me, pulled by a scrawny young boy that let out a *whoop* to warn me. I shifted back to let him pass.

Out of the corner of my eye, a flash of bright blue came to my right. A witch with light blond hair at the roots, tapering to a dark brown at the bottom and underneath, strode by. Her eyes caught mine. She frowned, then stepped into a store and disappeared. The bright blue color I'd seen had been the sparkle of a barrette, pulling her hair back over her right ear.

The warmth inside me stirred.

Startled, I blinked several times. Who was that? Why did her differently-colored hair remind me of Ava? The god magic inside me had come to life near her, but once I could no longer see her, the heat in my blood settled.

"Outta the way! Ya gonna get trampled, all right?"

A bellowing voice shook me from my thoughts. I shot a glare back to the witch shouting at me from atop a horse and pressed into the pub. My cloak billowed behind me as I ignored the patrons and headed toward the back. A set of sharp, twirling stairs that smelled like someone had attempted to clean them with vinegar soap led to the third floor, where I stepped off.

Thoughts of the strange witch shook out of me as I walked. A few doors down, I stopped and lifted my hand to knock. It opened before I could touch the wood. Merrick smiled at me, his brilliant, hazel eyes warm in the cool hallway.

"B," he murmured.

"Merrick."

The door opened wider. "Come in," he said. "I thought I saw you standing in the street, the vague figure in a dark cloak."

With a chuckle, I pushed the hood off and stepped inside. My gaze roamed the interior as he closed the door.

Warmth met me. Despite the downtown sham of Chatham City outside, the room was respectably kept. Updated, even. Wooden floors, a small fireplace with a chimney that issued directly outside. Made bed, a dresser, and plenty of light from long windows.

"Nice place."

Merrick drew in a deep breath, his shoulders expanding. "Thanks. It's . . . surprisingly quiet."

Indeed, the room held less noise than I'd expected. With all of Chatham City at his feet now, I expected a lot more din. I slipped over to the windows and peered out. Indeed, the chaos unfurled below, but no sound of it lingered inside.

The witch with the barrette had also disappeared.

"Silencing incantations?" I asked.

"A must," he said with a wry smile.

I returned the smile, then motioned to his desk. Ink bottles and quills sat on top of a pillow of half-opened parchments on a small desk. "The work of an Ambassador, I suppose?"

"Far less exciting than it sounds."

I laughed. He sounded entirely put-out about it. "Correspondence is *very* boring," I agreed. "It . . . it seems odd, doesn't it?"

"That I'm inside writing letters?"

"Well . . . yes."

"Unnatural," he agreed, with feeling. A wave of his hand toward Letum Wood followed. "I should be out there, with you, running."

"Much better plan," I murmured, but looked back out the window.

It's where we both belong, I wanted to say.

The last several months had seen a slow knitting back together of our friendship. His busy schedule, with my home in Letum Wood, led to not-often-enough meetings. The time we did have together held some reservation to it. A run in the forest. A quick dinner at a far-off inn near the outskirts of Chatham City or Ashleigh. Stolen time as friends. Neither of us wanted to break the fragile skein of whatever uncertainty lingered between us still.

"Well," I said, spinning one last time to encompass the place. "I'm glad you invited me to see it. For your sake, I'm also glad you moved out of the castle."

He laughed and sat on the edge of his bed, forearms braced on his thighs. "Yes, that place is a madhouse. I didn't mind it in the Wall when I was a Protector, but the political side?" His cheeks puffed as he blew out a breath. "Council Members and cleaning crews are up working all night, and surprisingly loud."

"Too busy." My nose wrinkled. "Much too busy. How is your . . . ah . . . project?"

A vague hesitation appeared on his face, and I hoped for something more to come of my question than his usual *nothing so far.* Merrick, as an Ambassador from the Northern Network, had a habit of being busy all the time.

Unsupportably busy.

He flittered around here and there to attend all the appropriate meetings, busied himself with getting to know the right witches, and tracking other Networks the way any self-respecting Ambassador would.

Yet, in the midst of all that, he *also* disappeared for unknown periods of time, returned with a black eye, bloody nose, and torn clothes. A few vague questions about Letum Wood, how much the trees were aware of, and whether the forest tracked witches who lived there had further set me on edge.

Whatever he did somehow tracked back to the death of their former High Priestess, Farah. The Northern Network Council announced her death of a severe fever only a few months after the War of the Networks.

Merrick had been on a Protector mission given by Papa at the time. A few days after her death, Merrick returned to me in the forest. We ended our relationship that evening so he could return to a shattered Network and a demanding Council.

That's all I could be certain of.

To my mind, Farah's death hadn't been a fever. My assumptions were my own, but he never denied them when I asked. Merrick was tracking the truth down now, I further assumed.

He called it his "project".

While he sought answers about the truth behind Farah's death, we remained in a careful dance of cordial friendship, living life around each other.

"The project is fine," he said, and a firm edge returned to his face. "Anyway, thanks for coming. Everything all right for you?"

His right eyebrow had risen and I cursed his ability to read me so well. "Fine," I said, but his skeptical expression pressed me to explain. "I just came from a meeting with Scarlett. The Council gave me five minutes to speak about the Sisterhood at the next Esbat."

He frowned. "Five minutes? It'll take Aldred that long to stop talking about himself."

"Right." I lowered onto a chair near his desk, pulling my lower lip through my teeth in thought. "But I suppose it's better than an outright denial."

"When is it?"

"In a week."

"Gives you time to prepare."

I nodded, "Which I think I'll need. I had an idea I wanted to run by you before I decide what to say to them, though."

"Sure."

"What can you tell me about Matthias? As a leader."

Curiosity overcame him next, but he set aside his questions to answer. "A natural-born Protector. His ability to focus on a problem and come up with ideas until the problem is solved is part of why I think he was instituted in Derek's place. Why?"

As briefly as I could, I told him about my discussion with Scarlett. The lines in his brow creased as he listened. When I mentioned getting Matthias's backing for the Sisterhood, he made a noise in his throat.

"What?" I asked. "What does that noise mean?"

Merrick frowned. "Well, for one, Scarlett is right. Don't tell Matthias that he needs help."

"His ego can't handle it?" I muttered, arms crossed over my middle.

"Not that, although maybe it's a little true, but it'll discredit you. Nothing in the current situation shows that he hasn't been handling matters in a capable way thus far. Like it or not, Bianca, you're making assumptions about the future and asking him to believe them."

"The demigods are here!" I cried.

"Show me one."

I scowled. "You know I can't. They look just like us, can

think their magic instead of requiring incantations, and might have been here for years, for all we know. It makes it almost impossible to find them. Our response to Bram would also mean that no demigod would be foolish enough to reveal themselves."

Merrick leaned his back against the wall. "Then explain to me how the Sisterhood will augment the Brotherhood. How are you going to help?"

"We aren't expected, for one. Most places in Alkarra won't allow women into their Guardian ranks, except the North. Neither witches or demigods would expect a woman to be ready to intercept whatever they're doing. We're fast, even if we aren't as physically strong as men. Plus, we think differently. We can go places men can't."

"Like?"

My ready words paused. This was good. He could ask me all these questions so I'd have my answers prepared. The problem?

I didn't yet have my answers prepared.

"Ah . . . brothels?"

He lifted the other eyebrow.

"All right, so men go to brothels!" I cried. "But there are lots of places where a woman would be trusted over a man. I just haven't been on a mission so I don't have specifics."

"Exactly." Merrick leaned forward. "You don't know what you don't know. Matthias isn't going to believe your word alone that something is needed. In his eyes, you're practically a child. The need for a Sisterhood is a realization he'll have to come to on his own."

"He might not."

Merrick shrugged. "Make it so he can't ignore you. You may have to . . . be a bit unconventional."

I blinked, mulling over that word. Unconventional, I could do.

"How?" I murmured. "The Sisterhood needs to be like the Brotherhood so that we can help each other and use the same funding, which sort of negates the unconventionality of it right away."

His eyes twinkled a bit when he said, "That's for the Head of the Sisterhood to know, isn't it?"

I smirked.

He grinned.

"Would the support of the Ambassador of the North be unconventional enough?" I asked.

His lips twitched. "If you're asking me to give my support for the Sisterhood, then you have it. One hundred percent. I'll stand behind it every day, in every way, and to anyone you want."

My heart fluttered. Friend or other, he could still disarm me with a smile and his wit. "Do you think Matthias would care if the Northern Network Ambassador supported me?"

Merrick laughed. "Not a bit."

"Why not? You're important *and* you were a Protector. Not to mention that you're also the Northern Network equivalent of a Protector. Matthias respects Regina and the Masters. Plus, the Masters are run by a woman! Regina is a powerful woman in my favor."

Merrick hesitated, and some of the hilarity faded from his eyes. His gaze dropped as he said, "He won't care about my opinion because of other reasons. Regardless, B, I think Scarlett has a point. It doesn't mean that you shouldn't approach Matthias. It just means that you should be prepared, and guard your expectations. It's unlikely Matthias will be willing to do anything for you right now."

A surge of unreasonable frustration followed what he said. I let it slide through me, startled when I felt a little quiver of fire with it.

God magic?

The stirring, so gentle, left as soon as it came. Perhaps I mistook it for something else, but my mind momentarily fluttered back to the witch I'd seen on the street.

"Thank you," I said with a long breath. "I appreciate the advice and the dose of reality."

His teeth flashed white when he gave me a fast smile. "You didn't believe Scarlett?"

"I did. I just . . . needed a second opinion. And to see your place."

"I'm glad you came," he said softly.

"Can I give you a housewarming gift? I found it in a grimoire on home decorating that Leda gave me in a sort-of-not-so-subtle way of telling me I needed to spruce up my cottage."

He laughed. "Please."

I gestured over to the door and sent a little spell. A strand of Letum ivy appeared there, growing in two lines on either side of the doorframe. Curly tendrils grew off the main one in flecks of green, the triangular leaves a mellow emerald, but bright at the same time. The vines thickened into a lush bush that crawled its way across the wall, filling the empty space. The mossy scent of Letum Wood followed.

The broad smile on his face made memorizing the individual spell and practicing it for three days worth it.

"It's perfect," he murmured. "I'll think of you every time I see it."

"It'll last a month," I said. "Call me when it's ready for a refresher and we'll try one with flowers."

"I promise."

Reluctantly, I headed for the door. Leaving Merrick always had a bittersweet twinge. Bitter because I enjoyed my time with him, but sweet because I didn't know how to navigate the waiting air between us. If nothing else, being his friend felt like coming back home.

Merrick leaned one shoulder against the doorway as I slipped out. His lazy smile and the easy way he held his body made my heart flutter.

"Good to see you, Mer," I murmured.

"You too, B."

With that, I headed toward the stairs, the heat of his gaze hot on my back the whole way down.

Chapter Two

I thought of almost nothing but speaking to Matthias.

While Ava sat with Priscilla at my table and read out loud from a small child's textbook, I contemplated whether the Network really *did* need the Sisterhood.

As I jogged through the snowy forest, my mind plotted out what details I'd tell Matthias. My skills. Timeline. Potential candidates—not that I had any yet, but they couldn't be that hard to find.

While I combed through the Southern Network in a fruitless search for signs of demigods, I imagined how a written proposal might start.

Could I leave such a proposal behind for him to consider later?

Worth a shot.

One thing rang true: Merrick and Scarlett had been right. I couldn't approach Matthias without a plan.

Slowly, a proposal for the Sisterhood cobbled together in my mind. Imperfect, of course. Probably riddled with leaking holes that I couldn't see, but I memorized it until I knew every angle possible.

Three days after asking Scarlett and Merrick what they thought, I slipped into a clean, periwinkle blue dress with an underskirt of gray, laced my boots all the way to my knees, ran a bone-comb through my hair, and transported to the Wall.

* * *

The Head of Protectors and Head of Guardians shared an office at the Gatehouse, which sat on top of the Wall.

It hovered above the portcullis where Chatham road spilled into the upper bailey. The view gave both leaders the ability to scan for incoming trouble or intruders, and a quick response time to issues within the castle.

The Gatehouse was split into three rooms, an office on either side and a shared common space in the middle. When Papa was Head of Protectors and I lived at Chatham Castle, I'd visit Tiberius, the former Head of Guardians, and laugh at his inappropriate jokes told in a baritone voice. He pretended not to like me, when adoration ran deep.

As I headed there now, several years older and with more experience, I felt a giddy rush. Like I was still a young girl who couldn't wait to find her place amidst Papa's peers. The Protectors had always loved my spirit and skill with a sword.

I hoped that meant something today.

Two Guardians slipped out of the Gatehouse and headed toward me as I approached the door. One of them lit up when they recognized me. Arther and Nelson, whom I recognized as recruits I'd trained two years ago.

"Gentleman," I murmured.

"Miss Monroe," they intoned, synced together. One of them grinned foolishly as they passed, and the other laughed. I rolled my eyes. Many Guardians openly joked about having a crush on me, and argued who would win my attention in a battle of swords, but I always ignored their jests.

Below us, the main doors were open and the portcullis drawn. Witches from Chatham City walked in and out of a market in the upper bailey. Chickens clucked, flapping noisily in cages while their owners called over the ruckus. Goats protested being tied up, and a few young cows bucked around a pen made of wood. Clothes fluttered in a cool breeze. Despite the snow yesterday, the air felt fresh instead of cold.

Months ago, vendors from all over Alkarra would have been here. Witches would have packed into the lower and upper bailey, filling every available space.

Now, the half-full market looked desolate. Networks had been restricting travel across borders ever since the Celebration, and it felt an awful lot like the required isolation of the Mansfeld Pact had started to return.

The idea of closing borders made my stomach hurt. After the three years of freedom to travel and meet other witches, I sincerely hoped tenuous Network relations didn't come to that.

The market faded behind me as I stopped at the Gatehouse door, where a male witch eyed me. Tysen, a new Protectors recruit that had been working with the Brotherhood for the last few months.

He tilted his head toward the door in subtle acceptance. I sent him a quick wink that he didn't return, but he did nudge me with a firm elbow as I passed by.

When I stepped inside, a flood of memories barreled toward me. I hadn't come into the Gatehouse since Papa left it to become High Priest.

Was that four years ago now?

Not much had changed since then. On the right, the Head of Guardians' office contained a sprawling table large enough to seat all the Captains. Outside the office, a fire burned in the hearth. Smaller tables cluttered the wall in the open space, some of them littered with crumbs and an old set of the table game: *Networks*.

On the left waited Matthias's office. A quiet, subtle place. Smaller than the Head of Guardians and sparse of decorations. Matthias sat inside, near the fire along the wall. The sight of him sent a rush of anxiety through me.

He sat near the fire behind a modest desk, reading a scroll. Sunlight slanted through the windows, illuminating the room with a smoky light. I stopped in the doorway, gathering my courage.

He glanced up, saw me, and blinked. He tossed the scroll into the fire.

"Bianca," he drawled.

"Merry meet."

Like most Protectors, Matthias was a daunting witch. He kept his hair cut short, cropped near his head. He had skin dark as night, with eyes as intense. Shoulders cut a broad figure as he stood up, wearing the half-armor that Papa rarely parted with when he was Head of Protectors. An underlying fatigue lingered in Matthias' eyes.

"Does your father need me?" he asked, his voice like rolling thunder.

"Ah, no. I came for myself. Do you have a few minutes to talk?"

He hesitated only a beat before he nodded and motioned to a chair on the other side of the fire.

I couldn't help but wonder how he perceived my arrival. Strange? Unwelcome? Another chair materialized across from the one I lowered into, this one much bigger. He sat in it, and I sensed wariness in his movements.

"So," he purred, like a panther in the Saltu jungle of the East. "What can I do for you?"

"I came to talk to you about forming a Sisterhood of Protectors to work alongside the Brotherhood."

His expression didn't waver. I fought to maintain the silence that followed my statement. Filling it with more words would only make me appear nervous.

"A Sisterhood?" he finally murmured.

I nodded.

He leaned powerful arms onto his knees, which were bent in front of him. His feet had planted on the floor, at least twice the size of mine in a pair of leather shoes that tied at the ankle.

"Why?" he asked.

Sensing what might be my only real opening, I responded with the words that I'd been practicing for days.

"I want to help with the demigod problem . . . and all the problems that may follow. There's never been a Sisterhood, not in recorded history, and I think it's a good time for one."

He leaned back. "Why?"

"Because we face an unconventional enemy," I murmured. "And sometimes that requires an unconventional edge."

Although he posed no threat to me—Matthias would never harm me—I could feel animosity behind his thoughts.

"And you want to be that unconventional edge?"

"No," I replied. "Women *are* that unconventional edge."

He chuckled, but it had little humor. The arguments I had given Merrick seemed weak now. Yes, women could get into places that men couldn't, but Protectors were highly trained with magic and transformation. Any place that required a woman meant a Protector would simply transform into a woman, among other things.

Matthias studied me. "You're serious?"

"Yes."

His gaze tapered. "How would you train?"

"Just like you."

"You would train with the Protectors?"

"If you let us."

He laughed again, this time a mocking sound. I clenched my teeth together as he slowed. Matthias shook his head.

"Bianca," he murmured chidingly, "be serious. Women are not as strong as men. We have advantages you don't."

My nostrils flared. Instead of rising to the bait—perhaps he wanted to goad me into an emotional reaction to prove women were too *emotionally labile* for this kind of work—I let out a steady breath and bunched my hand into a fist. The bite of my nails into my palm grounded me.

"I learn fast," I said. "I'm quick with a sword and talented with magic. I've already seen battles. I was kidnapped by Mabel and made it out of captivity in the Western Network alive. I'm accustomed to crossing borders and interacting with other witches, cultures, and languages. Most of all, my father has been training me my whole life. Maybe not intentionally for me to start a Sisterhood, but it's in my blood."

He didn't roll his eyes, but I had a feeling he wanted to. His wide nostrils flared, a sure sign of agitation. My window of opportunity began to narrow. I could feel it sliding away.

"We can do things differently," I said quickly. "Women have different talents than men."

"Please," he drawled, "enlighten me. How are we not doing things well enough for you?"

"I didn't say that."

His gaze never wavered, but I sensed a building pressure behind it.

"Women are more easily trusted than men, and we think differently," I said. "We might bring different ideas or magic types to the Network. Instead of physical brawn, we might think of other ways to approach a mission."

"You think we're closed-minded."

"Yes."

The retort came out of me before I could stop it. Despite the tightening of his lips, I couldn't regret saying the truth.

Wasn't this whole conversation proof that the Brotherhood didn't think outside the norms? Hadn't they operated the same way for decades now?

"There is a reason women aren't allowed in the Protectors or the Guardians," he said, drawing himself up. "We are physically superior and stronger. That makes a difference in battle."

"Your argument is invalid," I said calmly. "I fought in the War of the Networks, particularly at the Battle of Chatham Castle. I survived Mabel. Even managed to escape her ridiculous prison in the Western Network. I survived losing my magic, a demigod attack, and receiving my goddess magic back. My experience is powerful, Matthias. You can't deny that."

"It's still different."

"How?"

"You'd die on your first mission. Another man would come along and physically defeat you."

"They didn't during the Battle of Chatham Castle."

"Merrick fought with you."

"He didn't walk around saving me," I muttered, teeth clenched. "He was keeping himself alive as well. We fought together, and he'd be the first to tell you that."

Matthias shrugged. "We can't prove that and his opinion doesn't matter here."

We can, I thought. Hiddleston, a Defender who used magic to see the past, could go back to that terrible night. He could prove that Merrick wasn't my bodyguard, that I had prowess in battle.

But would it even matter?

"Because I needed physical strength when I defeated Mabel, did I?" I snapped.

"Your father defeated Mabel, Bianca."

I opened my mouth to speak, but he'd stunned me into

silence. My lips bobbed back to a close. I recoiled, stung. How did he have the courage to say that to my face?

In factual terms, I couldn't dispute it. Physically, Papa had overcome Mabel. I had been the distraction that enabled him to do so. I'd re-entered Mabel's mind in the final moments of the Battle of Chatham Castle and turned her attention. With that gap in her attention, Papa delivered the killing blow. Mabel died with me at her side.

My nostrils flared as I replayed what he'd said, struck to my core. My hands started to shake.

What response could I possibly give? One of his dark brows rose slightly, as if he realized what he'd said.

He didn't take it back.

"That's how you see it?" I whispered, gaunt.

He spread his hands, as if to show me all the facts. "That is how it *was*, Bianca. Yes, you provided some distraction to buy your father time, but the victory was his. He destroyed the Almorran Master and then the magic. While important, you were not instrumental. The Sisterhood would likely be the same. Is it worth the work and the sacrifice when you could impact the Network positively in other ways?"

My heart shriveled inside of me.

While important, you were not instrumental.

Even worse was that I could sense his sincerity. He really believed this to be true. Did the rest of the Protectors have the same mindset? The Network?

Did I have an inflated sense of the service I'd given for my witches?

Embarrassment flooded me.

This had gone wrong, and not even for the reasons I'd expected. There was no way to prepare for such a rebuttal. No response I could give that would make any difference at all. Matthias had decided himself against me before he knew my plan existed.

Matthias stood and put a hand on my shoulder. It felt heavy, like a weight, and warm. His words sent rage all the way through my bones.

"You're fighting a fight you cannot win, Bianca. I care too much for you to see you go through all this pain and frustration for nothing. The distraction a Sisterhood would provide while we search for the demigods would harm our Network, not help it. Women were not made for this work. My words come from a place of care for you. Put your focus elsewhere."

I stood and shoved his arm off of me as hard as I could.

He reared back, startled.

"Do not touch me again without my permission," I whispered, fury strengthening my voice. "I am a woman, *not* a child. One day, you will respect me as the Head of the Sisterhood and you will address me as such. This unprecedented war requires unprecedented answers. I will be that answer with or without you. I would never willingly make an enemy of you, Matthias. I would ask you not to do the same."

We stared at each other, wordless, until my pattering heart threatened to explode. My cape fluttered around my legs as I turned and headed for the door. His voice stopped me as I reached for the rope that pulled it open.

"Don't do this, Bianca. If you really want to help your witches, then you will focus on other things."

I drew in a deep breath, but refused to look at him.

"One day," I said calmly, "when the Sisterhood saves your life, you will remember this exact moment."

The door slammed shut behind me.

* * *

My blood boiled as I transported to Letum Wood.

The moment my feet hit the snowy earth, I darted away. While running, I issued a spell. My cloak loosened, then fluttered in the air behind me. I sent it home with a different incantation. The Volare bounced out of the case where I housed it on my back and took to the air, darting ahead. It had been cooped up for hours now, and loved to stretch itself in the woods.

I ran.

I ran until my lungs threatened to burst. Until the heat and the fury and the fire burned low. An hour passed, maybe two. I lived in the painless moments between breaths, when the running became smooth and my thoughts too full to think and reality so far behind me, I didn't have to see it.

When my body began to hurt, I slowed.

Then stopped.

The quiet of Letum Wood filled the air around me as I stood in between two tree roots taller than my head. I leaned back against them. The moment I touched them, a melodic voice sang in my mind.

You belong to us.

I closed my eyes.

"I do," I whispered.

The croon turned into a happy melody, a hum that filled my soul and cleaned out all the cobwebs. Letum Wood had always been my only safe place. The place where the magicks inside me never fought.

Where I could trust my spells, my heart, my soul.

Weary now, I leaned back more fully. Anticipating my thought, the Volare zipped up behind me, catching me before I hit the ground.

"Let's explore," I murmured.

The Volare hovered above the ground with me on top, slowly working its way through the forest. My heart slowed as I watched the underside of the canopy pass overhead. Eventually, I climbed off to walk.

Aimlessly, we wandered the forest, searching for signs of

life. Snow lay sparse here. Much of it didn't make it past the thick canopy of branches overhead. Inches would pile on branches above, while only a skiff made it to the ground.

When my beating heart slowed, I wiped the sweat off my brow with a shake of my head. At my command, the Volare rolled itself back into a tight ball and returned to the container on my back.

The initial disbelief over my conversation with Matthias had faded into a low-burning rage.

There was one other witch that might mirror my outrage. A witch I needed to talk to so I could get this frustration out of my head.

* * *

As a perk for returning to her position as Head Assistant for Scarlett, Leda negotiated for a better living space at Chatham Castle.

Not only was it located closer to the High Priestess's office, but it had a separate bedroom and living area. While still not large, she had more area than my cottage in Letum Wood and shelves to organize her many scrolls and books.

When I knocked on her door a few minutes later, a flurry of noises came from inside. Voices, mostly.

Leda, for one. She sounded . . . forceful. A male voice, for another. Before I could press my ear to the wood, the door breezed open. Leda stood there, gaze burning, neck high with a flush. The reason revealed itself a second later when Hiddleston stood from a ratted divan near the fireplace.

My eyes widened.

"Not," Leda muttered darkly, "a word."

Her arm extended straight out as she pushed the door farther open, then stepped back. As if on command, Hiddleston headed toward us. His placid expression revealed little, but a glimmer of amusement gave him away.

They'd been debating again.

Hiddleston had likely dropped in on Leda, unannounced, and wheedled into her room with a well-sculpted debate point. This was a recurring event now, despite Leda's insistence that *we aren't friends.*

"Bianca," he murmured as he passed.

"Hiddleston."

The smell of cloves followed as he strode into the hall and left without looking back. He'd gathered his long locks into a wide queue at the base of his neck, and they flared out over his shoulders.

I watched him go, bemused.

Leda grabbed my arm, yanked me inside, and shut the door with more force than necessary. She spun on her heel and paced toward the far wall, which had several high windows across the top. Muted light streamed through them. I bit back the urge to cough. One of the fireboys needed to check her chimney.

"So," I drawled, "how is Hiddleston?"

She sent me a wrathful glare as I settled on the divan where Hiddleston had been sitting. A cast-off from Marten's office. Leda had always been prompt with repurposing anything. Nicknacks ringed the walls on wooden shelves she'd secured to the stone with spells. Extra quills, parchment, ink bottles. She never got rid of any item that held a hope of use.

She held onto her arms behind her back as she paced back and forth by a low, square table.

"I don't want to talk about Hiddleston," she snapped.

On the floor in front of the divan lay a clue. A sheaf of papers rustled there, stirred from a gentle draft that snuck under her door.

"What are these?" I asked.

She blew an exasperated raspberry and jabbed a finger toward them. "*Those*," she muttered, "are the reason he came."

I spelled the collected papers onto my lap. They were perfectly rectangular, cut to the same size, and flat. A rare find in a world of curling parchments that formed whatever size they formed. Most parchment mills kept a general shape for their scrolls, but nothing consistent. Only special orders—and the very wealthy—could afford pages like this.

"Looks important," I said.

She huffed, but watched me out of the corner of her eye as I continued to peruse, grateful to get my mind off Matthias.

Each page contained two columns of words. On the left, at the very top, was a calligraphic form of the words *Mortal Court: Declan*. On the right was the same style of letters, but the words *Current Day: Muran*.

The Muran system was our current language and magical system, which meant these papers had something to do with language. Coming from Hiddleston, a powerful Defender that could see the paths of the past and how they laid out, was a very interesting lure.

Below each title was a list of words. Twenty entries per page. At the bottom middle of each paper was a page number. The pages were all handwritten in order. In the back, they held conjugated verb stacks, eight per page. With each page I turned, the answer played itself out in bolder terms.

Oh, Hiddleston. Wily witch indeed.

He'd created a book-ready translation reference for Leda. She could study Declan as it was spoken thousands of years ago in the mortal courts and compare it to our language today. Not only would this help her with Ava—a little—but it spoke to her deep love of history. This was fluff. It had nothing to do with their occasional professional collaborations together.

He'd pegged her weakness completely.

"Do you see my conundrum?" Leda asked, lips pinched and voice too high. "Do you see what he's done?"

I cleared my throat to buy myself another moment of thought.

"Based on what I see," I said slowly, "I'm assuming that Hiddleston has been working in the paths to learn the Declan language as spoken in the mortal courts, back when the mortals and witches lived together. He's been transcribing what he finds to make this extremely organized, alphabetized list of words and verb conjugations."

When I lifted my questioning gaze to her, she nodded.

"And he has the nerve to allow you to study it?" I ventured carefully.

The rigid lines on her face eased a little. Her shoes made a *tapping* sound as she came over to my side, settled down, and sighed.

"No."

"What did I get wrong?"

"He's not allowing me to study it. He . . . he *gave* it to me."

I rolled my lips to hide a smile. Hiddleston, over the past months, had proven to be a surprising witch. Although clearly interested in Leda, he'd stopped his most obvious pursuit tactics once Scarlett re-appointed her as her Head Assistant. He worked for Papa and Scarlett, bouncing around as Papa needed his Defender skills and Scarlett his language translation skills.

His first move had been on her emotional guards.

As occasional Assistant to the High Priestess, Hiddleston had settled into a keeping-at-arms length position with Leda. The space allowed her ample room to get used to him. Leda had assumed her old position with Scarlett, and he helped with the translations Scarlett required. He was prompt, willing, and easy to work with.

His second move had been on her social guards.

Every now and then, he'd given a quiet sign of friendship. He'd leave a book that she'd been trying to find, stay late to help her finish a work project, or bring her favorite dinner for all the Assistants when meetings went long.

Meanwhile, she'd been free to take a deep breath of relief and settle into her job. All that time, he may have just been readying himself.

Had his final move to officially court her begun?

I couldn't wait to find out.

Leda frowned, and it marred the porcelain effect of her pale skin. She really needed to get outside more.

"It . . . it muddies things when he's kind for no reason like that, and with something that must have taken a while."

"So you're angry with him?"

The back of her neck grew pinker. "Angry is not the right word. Though," she murmured, "I might have come on a bit too strong when I tried to give it back and insisted I wouldn't take it. He didn't listen. I just . . . I don't trust him."

"Why not?"

"I don't know!" she cried. "Because it's hard to think through my arguments around him. He anticipates things and that infuriates me."

"Oh," I drawled. "So he's the only male you can't boss around entirely?"

Her withering glare drew a laugh out of me.

"What?" I cried. "It's true."

Leda waved toward the parcel of papers. "This sort of gift is too much. It's . . . this must have taken him weeks. Months!"

"He might be interested in advancing our ability to communicate with demigods," I said. "Assuming any other mortals or demigods are found in Alkarra, of course. And that they speak this ancient version of Declan, which they don't. Does that soften the blow for you?"

Her jaw tightened for a moment. "I hadn't thought of that," she murmured. "Perhaps he has Network interests in mind."

"Not everything is about you."

She sent me another scathing look in response. "I don't think that, thank you very much. Being the oldest of who-knows-how-many-children now, I know it is never about me, Bianca." Her shoulders expanded in a deep breath. "You're right. I may be reading too much into his offering. The nice paper, the organization, the presentation . . ."

Her voice wandered off for a moment, and her focus went with it. I let her inhabit those strange roads for a few more seconds before she snapped out of it on her own. With another little huff, she took the papers from me.

"Did you need something?" she asked imperiously.

The story of Matthias and my massive embarrassment hovered on the tip of my tongue, but I swerved at the last moment. Her current frame of mind would be the worst time to approach Leda. I never knew what she'd say when Hiddle-ston had her feathers ruffled.

"Is Ava here?" I asked. "She didn't come for breakfast this morning."

"No." Leda set aside the papers and patted a piece of hair out of her eyes. "She was with Baxter in your father's office yesterday morning, last I saw her."

"Oh."

She arched an eyebrow. "Why do you ask?"

"Just needed to ask her something about amulets." I shook my head. "Come to my place tonight? Priscilla is cooking now that she can tolerate smells again. Fina had some ginger left-over from this summer's herb garden. She made Priscilla a tonic and said it should help her keep food down."

Leda ruminated, then nodded once. "Yes, as long as Priscilla is cooking. Thank you."

I ignored the subtle jab as a scroll appeared. A common occurrence these days, now that Leda ran Scarlett's life. Absently, Leda tapped on the seam. It began to unroll itself, dividing her attention.

"Oh," I added as an aside, my voice oddly strangled, "I think I just made an enemy of Matthias when I told him that I basically have a revenge plot against him."

Unfazed, Leda perused the scroll.

"Why?" she murmured.

"I presented the idea of the Sisterhood to him," I continued. "I asked for his endorsement."

Her hazel-and-green eyes tapered to slashes, then opened back up with a blink. The scroll still dangled in the air when Leda peeled herself away from it, hands on her hips, head tilted to the side.

"For what purpose?" she asked. Her inquisitive tone was absolutely neutral.

"Public support before I go to the Council," I said. "They allowed me a measly five minutes at the next Esbat. I thought if Matthias stood behind the idea, the Council would as well. I spent the last three days preparing and . . . anyway, it didn't go well."

My cheeks heated, but the ire had eased. In these declining moments after my run, my muscles began to tighten and I felt tired.

Her brow rose. "Do you need his approval?"

The question gave me pause. An overwhelming *yes!* overtook my mind, but I forced myself to question it. Leda wouldn't have asked that question if there wasn't a side door answer I hadn't yet considered.

"Why wouldn't it help?" I asked instead.

"That didn't answer my question. Do you need his approval?"

"Well . . . maybe?"

She rolled her eyes. "What would Matthias publicly acknowledging a Sisterhood do for you in front of the Council?"

"Pressure them to accept the idea more quickly. They only gave me five minutes."

"Because you didn't listen to me," she said archly. "The agenda was full for this Esbat, Bianca. You have to find one that has wiggle room. They just started to take witch appeals again, which means *everyone* is trying to talk to them." She waved a hand in the air. "They're still dealing with all the Celebration nonsense. More time could open up for you in a few months."

"They're booked for a year!"

She shrugged. "These things require patience."

Her almost-verbatim response from Scarlett's nearly made my teeth grind. The demigods were most likely here now. We could shortly find ourselves in a desperate position where we needed a new strategy, but . . . I wasn't about to get into that debate with her. Not now. My legs were shaky from the too-long run and I needed food.

"Fine," I murmured. "I'll . . . figure something else out."

Leda's tone softened. "I'm sorry, Bianca. I didn't mean to scold you. Tell me what he said. I really do want to know."

I gazed at her, startled by the shift. Leda rarely apologized. "Really?"

"Really."

By the time I finished the retelling, the self-righteous indignation I'd hoped to see didn't fail me. Leda stood stiff as a pillar near the fire.

"Well," she said, rage in her voice. "The absolute nerve of that man! I can't wait for you to make that a reality. In due process of time," she added as a calmer aside.

Telling her about it did make me feel better. While the

burning rage of injustice still brightened my chest, I could relax a little more now.

"Thanks for listening," I said. "I feel better."

She nodded. "Of course. I'll try to think of a few other options. Taken in the context of what you just told me, maybe Matthias *is* what you need to get Council support. Certainly wouldn't hurt, but . . . maybe there are other ways."

Leda trailed into thought, then shook out of it.

"I'll keep an eye open and let you know if I notice anything," she said. "In the meantime, don't do anything stupid, all right? You'll do yourself no favors by trying to show your skills and getting half-killed in the meantime."

"Thanks Mama," I said wryly.

She rolled her eyes. "That," she stated, "is one title I will never hold. Now, please leave. I need to write a thank you note to Hiddleston and get back to work. I'll see you this evening for dinner."

Chapter Three

The gardens at Chatham Castle lay in a strange silence when I strolled through them.

A restless night left me weary as I hurried through the blunted morning light, castle-bound. My head felt stuffy and slow, filled with dreams of trying to outrun Matthias through Letum Wood. Moments before I caught up to him, I'd jerk awake, sweaty and gasping.

A message received this morning from Marten ran through my mind. *Have breakfast with me, please?* it said. *I haven't seen you in a few days.*

I looked forward to sitting in his cozy office, which would be warm despite glass-pane windows. He'd have a pot of tea on a cast-iron arm to stay hot in the gentle flames, ready to sip and banish the chill morning.

Strands of frozen grass crunched beneath my feet as I shuffled through a garden filled with bushes no taller than my knee. The scraggly things had sturdy, deep umber leaves all winter long. Each sculptured bush had been designed by the gardeners to resemble snowflakes, expertly trimmed with stunning detail and facets. In the summer, they blossomed into butter-yellow flowers called *fairy tears*, each as soft as cotton puff.

Small, circular berries bloomed on them around Yule in collections of four. Their medicinal properties made them important for apothecaries—but difficult to grow just right—so this garden was protected by spells that prevented most witches from seeing it.

My grandmother, Hazel, had a hidden grove of such bushes not far from the house I grew up in, in the Bicker's Mill Coven. Memories of collecting the white berries as a little girl filtered through my mind as I strode past them.

Fortunately, the gardeners at Chatham knew me from when I collaborated with them about Letum Wood—the forest had a way of growing *everywhere*, even onto castle grounds—and allowed me access to the area. To any other witch, it appeared as nothing more than a field of grass.

While I strode through the field of living sculptures, a rustle of movement registered not far away. I slowed down as Papa appeared ten paces from me, sweat streaking his temples. His shoulders rose and fell quickly, as if he'd been running. He doubled over, hands on his thighs.

"Papa?"

His head jerked up, startled to see me. He blinked twice, then straightened.

"Morning, B."

Quickly, I closed the remaining space between us. My cloak fluttered as I moved, stopping a few paces away. His dark brown hair was a bit long these days, nearly brushing the tops of his ears. A days' growth of stubble shadowed his strong jaw, meaning he'd been out for a while.

"Everything all right?" I drawled. "You look a bit winded, old man."

He rubbed his hands together to generate warmth in his

fingers as I lifted an eyebrow. His cheeks puffed as he blew warm air into them.

"Just a morning demigod encounter," he said. "That's all."

The back of my neck prickled in a sudden rush of concern, taking my sleepy state away all at once. "What?"

"Demigod."

"I heard that," I muttered. "What's going on?

He glanced at me, then over his shoulder. Beyond the gardens and a side entrance to the castle not far away was Chatham City. He turned back around to face me, his fast breaths slowing into a normal pace.

"I chased a demigod just now."

"Where?"

He cleared his throat, then tilted his head toward the castle in a gesture. Wordless, I followed. We walked side-by-side, moving slowly. All the open area around us, combined with the deeply cold morning, meant no visible gardeners or witches lingered to overhear.

"I had an idea I wanted to test," he said. "Most of the Brotherhood were on assignments already, and I couldn't find Merrick yesterday afternoon."

"So you went yourself?"

A quick grin slipped over his face, robbing the obvious fatigue. I had my suspicions that he'd been out all night on this *assignment.*

"Maybe," he said.

Curiosity drove my next question. "Do you ask Merrick to still go on missions?"

He kept his gaze straight ahead. "Don't know what you're talking about," he said lightly. A bit *too* nonchalant. "Merrick is the Northern Network Ambassador, B. Why would he go on assignments from the Central Network?"

"Because you never officially released him from the Brotherhood."

"Only in death," Papa murmured.

"Right," I drawled. "That whole once-a-Brother-always-a-Brother motto is intact?"

Another answering smile.

The revelation that Merrick might still be an active Protector startled me a little. In his usual way, Papa confirmed nothing, so Merrick may not be active. The implications if Merrick were ever caught on a mission for Papa could be catastrophic politically for both Networks. Merrick had been so focused on the demigod issue anyway, I doubted he worked for the Protectors.

Still . . .

I shook those thoughts off for the more pertinent question. "And what did you find on your little adventure?"

His expression sobered. "Riddle me this logic, will you? Demigods are presumably here, correct?"

"Correct."

"And if they're here, they want something."

"Power and acclaim."

He snapped two fingers. "No, that's what they want in *Alaysia*. Alkarra will have a specific target for them to get said power and acclaim. Don't mistake their motivation for a goal."

"Fair enough."

We continued our slow saunter as Papa folded his hands behind his back, breath fogging in front of him.

"Bram came to Alkarra from Alaysia and immediately integrated himself as a leader. He was eventually able to rise to the level of High Priest. The Northern Network had an issue with a demigod named Jote. Jote also set himself up as a leader, but he wanted to overthrow the North. Even Baxter works with leadership," Papa murmured with greater thought, "though he isn't attempting a coup of the Central Network after more than three years."

"Nor attempting to lead himself."

"Fair point. Regardless, the pattern is there. Niko has some underground issues with a demigod that I won't go into now."

"Which leaves the West?"

"Precisely. I wanted to see if I could find a demigod in the West, near the Arck. They're clearly interested in integrating into Networks and attempting a takeover. Perhaps we can anticipate their next attempt."

The Arck was the Western Network castle, a structure of red rock and hidden waterfalls, ringed by a sandy, desert vista. My upper lip curled at the memories of my time there, kidnapped by Mabel years ago. A beautiful Network.

An ugly history.

"Why there?"

He shrugged. "A hunch. Demigods have attempted two long-term overthrows, maybe they'll do something more short-term."

"An attack."

"Yes. It's certainly a different approach, and it's what I would try in their shoes. A full attack. Takeover. Since we have Baxter and no signs of any obvious demigod in our midst, the West is the next most likely place to go. So I observed. Several times," he tacked on.

I sent him a sidelong glance as we passed a naked orange tree, but he acted as if he didn't notice.

"This isn't your first time?"

"No."

"And?"

"I found one."

He said it so rationally that I had a hard time knowing what to say next. Fortunately, he continued before I had to find the words, but a gentle shimmer settled around us, barely visible. A spell meant to prevent listening ears.

"A male," Papa continued. "He looked just like a Western

Network witch except for a collection of small gems on a leather bracelet on his left wrist. Reddish in color."

"A son of Ignis, then," I murmured.

Papa nodded and stopped again. "He was observing the castle, dressed like a West Guard, only the sash they wear across their bare chest on certain guard assignments was wrong in hue. Just slightly—the color was a little too pale. I confirmed my suspicion when he disappeared but left no magical signature. I couldn't follow his magic."

Transportation spells left a vague something behind, almost like an aura. Skilled witches like Papa could detect and follow such a trail. No other goddess magic existed in Alkarra to allow a witch to transport, so the spells were easy to identify.

God magic, however, left no magical signature. The inability to follow a demigod after they disappeared was a hallmark sign of god magic.

One of the few we could be certain of.

If the demigod used magic to disappear and Papa attempted to follow, that meant Papa had been *very* close to the demigod. Deciding not to ask those details, I instead said, "That confirms he was a demigod."

Papa nodded. "Then," he added, as an aside, "*I* was nearly detected by a West Guard, evaded that problem, then thought I saw the demigod in a market and I had to run after him to avoid being caught by the West Guards. Lana wouldn't have minded, but I couldn't deal with the time delay. The demigod saw me at one point and disappeared entirely. That's when I returned."

Papa rubbed his thumb along his bottom lip in thought. For several seconds, he stared at the castle with a heavy brow, then shook his head.

"Infuriating," he muttered. "It's so simple for them to get away. How are we supposed to fight such an easy escape?"

"We aren't," I murmured. "What did he look like?"

"Very pale, white skin. Brown hair, like mine." He gestured impatiently to his own hair. "Couldn't see his eye color. Slender. The amulet on his left wrist was a light leather-like material, with five red gems. Can't pinpoint *why* he drew my gaze, but . . ."

He trailed away.

Demigods had a strong *unknown* quality. An air of something intriguing that tended to lure witches to them out of sheer curiosity. Like a witch born with natural beauty and kindness that others couldn't stay away from.

"I think I saw a demigod in Chatham City the other day," I said. "Female with a blue barrette and two-toned hair, like Ava's. I didn't know she was a demigod, but her barrette caught my eye. She disappeared right after we made eye contact."

"Matthias thinks he found one in the Western Covens last week," Papa murmured. "But we haven't yet confirmed. They're certainly here, and clearly paying attention. The question we need to answer first is what is their big goal?"

Silence passed between us for several moments before he growled and ran a hand through his hair. It stood on end, slightly sweaty from his run. His fists flexed. "It's frustrating. Feels like I'm losing my touch when I can't get to the bottom of something like this."

"I'm sorry, Papa."

"They're wily, B." Amusement filled his tone, but it covered darkness underneath. "This is an enemy I'm not sure how to fight."

"Can you tell the Council that you saw a confirmed demigod in the West?"

"I can tell them," he said with exasperation, "but they won't believe it or do anything about it. Plus, Aldred would use it as an opportunity to stir witches back up. Say I had been shirking my High Priest duty, or something. Unless they can talk to the demigod and see physical proof, the Council is hesitant to truly believe the demigods are still here."

I rolled my eyes. "They're sticking their heads in the sand."

"I agree."

Papa made a noise in his throat that I couldn't decipher. The spell around us faded as we approached a side entrance, one that led to an old storage turret no one used. It required an extensive walk through Chatham to get to anywhere important, but the halls were lesser known and quiet, which made it worth it.

"Don't let me worry you, Bianca. I'm working on a plan to deal with all of this. It's a good plan. Unexpected, but sometimes that's what we need. I'll fill you in if it's needed. Let's be done with that. Everything all right with you?" he asked.

Matthias popped up in my head. While I wanted to tell Papa about the conversation yesterday, something held me back. Papa had his own troubles now. The Sisterhood was mine. As Highest Witch of the Central Network, he couldn't be part of my plans. In fact, he needed to be more distant than ever. If he hadn't been my father, I would have gone to *him* for endorsement.

The way things stood, I planned to do this on my own. Besides, Matthias would probably tell Papa himself.

"Yes," I said, "everything is fine."

He smiled and opened a creaky wooden door. Warmth infused his expression. "I'm always happy to see you. A better start to my day, for sure."

"Same, Papa. Sorry about the demigod. I'll keep an eye out around here."

He wrapped me in a warm embrace. "I need to get ready," he murmured, an eye on the clock. "I have a meeting with Aldred in twenty minutes. He's pushing back on my initiative to assign Central Guards at the main Southern Network markets."

"Why does Aldred care?" I asked, startled that Aldred would waste his time. "Inner-Network affairs are your responsibility, not his. He can't block the Highest Witch from taking action with the Guardians, Protectors, or other Network leadership."

He rolled his eyes. "Correct, but Aldred thinks everything I do is wrong. I plan to send eight, he wants me to send two. I normally don't have to haggle over Guardians. I command the Guardians and Protectors and it's done, just as I don't question their authority over inner-Network affairs to the same level. But Aldred stirs up trouble at every side."

"Sounds miserable."

He sighed. "Aldred just wants a more integrated Council and Highest Witch and I don't think it's a good idea. Scarlett is open to it, but she's not the Highest Witch. Anyway, it was Alina's request when four Southern Network women were attacked on their way home from the market."

"By Eastern Network witches?"

"The *Ilese* language was heard amongst them," Papa drawled, lips thin with annoyance, "but no identities have been confirmed."

"He can't stop you."

Papa frowned. "He shouldn't be able to," he murmured, "but that's part of the problem. He's been rallying other High Witches, Council Members, and even the *Chatham Chatterer* to discuss what I do. He tries to bring every detail to light, then overanalyzes it. Information about Network relationships that have never been discussed before are now in the *Chatterer*. Where I had trust, now I have none. Don't get me wrong—I think the Highest Witch should always have accountability. I will stand before my peers with pride because I have no decision I regret. But Aldred's inspection makes it almost impossible to act because he inflates every single aspect of it. It's tying up the decision-making process in the Council, which means important work isn't getting resolved or moved forward. Then he blames our current Highest Witch structure."

"Jikes," I muttered.

His recounting wasn't a surprise. I'd seen what Aldred had been doing for the last several months, and had to watch it happen helplessly on the side. Hearing the frustration in Papa's tone as he spoke about it, however, made it all too real.

"What about Scarlett?"

He sighed. "She's wisely maintained a politically-distant facade with me when we're out of my office, so the Council has a great deal more trust for her than me. The fact that she was a school teacher helps. The Teachers Guild endorsed her, which gave her some power. Regardless, she's a wonderful High Priestess."

I smiled. "I agree."

A distant expression showed on Papa's face for several long moments. "Don't worry, B." He blinked back to himself with a gentle smile. "We'll get through this."

I grinned. "We always do, Papa. Together."

"Together," he murmured.

His affectionate hug sent warmth through me. When he pulled away, I stepped back. "Good luck," I said. "Tell Aldred to drown himself in a teapot for me."

Papa snorted. "I taught you better insults than that. By the way, Baxter has been asking about you. Think he misses escaping to your cottage since Priscilla has been there."

I laughed and edged closer to the door. "He's been kicked out for now."

Papa's eyes crinkled at the edges with a smile. "That's right, B. Kick those boys out. You don't need them. None of them are good enough for you, anyway."

"Merry part, Papa. Love you."

The frustration in his expression softened.

"You too, B."

* * *

Later that day, the Chatham Chatterer newscroll flashed an unsurprising headline.

No Progress With Demigod Search.

Education Initiative Continues.

Similar sentiments had echoed for weeks now.

I studied the article and thought about my visit with Papa. His frustration had been palpable. Had he read this article? Marten would have opinions on it, certainly. As Ambassador, he and Baxter had worked together with the Teachers Guild to send witches into the most remote parts of Alkarra and educate them on the demigods, their intent, and how to notify leadership if they suspected they had seen one.

My thoughts fizzled into smoke when a plate of bread and smoked fish landed in front of me. A bulging eye in a lifeless, scaly fish head stared back. Priscilla's love of seafood hadn't ebbed since her pregnancy began, despite the awful smell. Now that Fina's ginger tonic had soothed her stomach, she ate ravenously.

"The education initiative was a brilliant suggestion on Scarlett's part," Priscilla said. She set a bowl of shelled leto nuts in front of me, the last of my fall harvest. "Not only to show that she drives real change for the Network, but to lessen the impact of the demigods."

I tapped the newsscroll and it rolled back together.

Priscilla settled on the stool across from me. Her dress hid the small bump that had been forming there the past several months. Though pale, her rampant exhaustion had faded slightly in the past few weeks. She hadn't been vomiting nearly as much as the days slid by.

"So you think the demigods are here?" I asked.

"They're fools if they aren't."

I mulled over that thought as I reached for a piece of bread. *Were* they fools if they stayed in their homeland, Alaysia? Ava had told us a little about life in their land, as much as she could with the lessening language barrier. She hadn't painted a clear picture beyond *really, really bad for mortals* and *not-so-bad for demigods*. Baxter, on the other hand, made it seem good.

For demigods.

Disparity muddied the water, and I had a feeling that the truth lay somewhere in the middle.

Once I removed the fish head and slit it open to the warm, cooked interior, I could stomach the food. I ate quickly while she chattered about her day, shucking bones off to the side. When natural conversation ebbed, I asked, "Any word from your parents?"

Her expression dropped. She pushed a few leto nuts around the plate and tried to hide her pain; she failed dramatically.

"No. To be fair, I haven't exactly reached out to them."

"Did they contact you when you lived in the East?"

She hesitated, then nodded. "Yes. Sometimes. At least, in the beginning. It tapered off as time passed."

I fought not to roll my eyes. Priscilla's wealthy parents rode the waves of whatever approval rating came next. Having their daughter as the fiancee of the Eastern Network High Priest had brought them a decent amount of socialite power at first.

Until Priscilla's handfasting never occurred.

After two years of an engagement that did not result in a wedding, Priscilla left Niko when he began to turn against the

Central Network and, by extension, against her. While other things derailed in Niko's life, his personality also dissolved. He became frustrated, sullen, and utterly withdrew from their relationship.

Now pregnant with his child, Priscilla fled the Eastern Network. A brief attempt to force her back hadn't ended well for Niko, and now Priscilla stayed with me. Daily, she spent time with Michelle, sometimes sleeping at her house for the night. Michelle's two young daughters helped Priscilla get an eye on what awaited her when the baby came.

I reached over and covered her hand with mine.

"I'm sorry, Priscilla."

A wobbly smile appeared on her face. Tears filled her bright green eyes, but she blinked them back.

"I think my parents are embarrassed that I never married Niko. The power I once offered them as the Eastern Network High Priestess is . . . well . . . entirely gone."

"Do you still miss Niko?"

"So much." A tear cascaded down her cheek, but she hastily wiped it away. "I miss what he was when we first found each other. The Niko of today is . . . vastly different. Anyway, the baby will be a welcome distraction soon."

Priscilla's pregnancy still hadn't been revealed to the general public. From what I understood of her plans, it wouldn't ever be. She planned to fade into life with Michelle and me until . . . well, until this situation played itself out. Having an heir to the Aldana dynasty was a powerful—or dangerous—thing. Until she could understand what it might mean, she'd exist here, with us, and take it a day at a time.

Not to mention the hostility against her from some pockets of the Central Network. Subdued, of course, and spoken of quietly. Plenty of witches here didn't trust her. Claimed she spied for Niko or gave away Network secrets or betrayed us by leaving in the first place.

She endured all this uncertainty while locked up tight in Letum Wood, not speaking a word to anyone but her friends. The child could be five or six before Priscilla stepped into the world with them, and I didn't blame her.

Thankfully, the forest welcomed Priscilla as one of mine, and strove to keep her as safe as it kept me. Somehow, the trees seemed to understand she carried a life inside her.

Her fingers squeezed mine. "I'm just grateful to have my friends." She laughed then, a bright sound at odds with the sorrow in her gaze. "Can you imagine? Years ago, at Miss Mabel's, we used to hate each other." A sad smile returned. "I'm grateful we've all grown up since then."

I smiled. "Me too. Any idea what you'll do after the baby comes? I mean," I added hastily, "there's no rush on my end. You're welcome here for as long as you want. It's nice having someone around."

Priscilla waylaid my fear with a wan smile. "Don't worry, Bianca. I feel very welcomed and at home here. Eventually, though, I *will* repay you and Michelle for all your kindnesses. Everyone brings me food and keeps me safe . . . one day, I'll pay it back." She paused here, brow wrinkled. "How? I have no idea right now. I think the path will come. Fina's elixir has helped me feel so much better, maybe I can focus on the other side of pregnancy."

An unexpected flare of god magic stirred in my blood like heat. I glanced up, startled, moments before a knock reverberated in the small room. Before I could stand, the door cracked open.

"Bianca?"

"Hey Bax." I relaxed against the seat. "Come in."

Baxter's roguish smile entered the room first. His head full of curly black locks, a well-fitting jacket over lean shoulders, and a pair of bright green eyes followed. He shut the door behind him with a little shiver, the tiny gems on his left wrist guard glimmering in the firelight.

"Cold," was all he said through clattering teeth.

His homeland, Alaysia, was reputedly a world of islands and heat. Nothing like the bitter, bone-deep cold the Central Network often produced. He'd struggled every winter, and now that I looked back, I could see why.

With a spell, Priscilla sent a few more logs onto the fire. I slid a chair out from under the table with my foot. "Have a seat. It's been a few days since I've seen you."

He sat with a heavy breath. Lines of fatigue tugged around the corners of his eyes, pulling them low. He'd single-handedly taken on coordinating the education of the Southern Network witches in remote areas, where demigods would be most likely to lure magicless witches into a lifelong agreement of servitude.

"Have you seen Ava today?" I asked. "I haven't seen her in days. She's been tricky to track down now that she'd learned the back halls and hidden passageways of Chatham Castle."

"Tell me about it," he muttered. "She's currently with your father." His brows rose, as if I should have known. "Of course."

I laughed. Papa and Ava had formed an interesting bond. More than once, I'd caught him teaching her sparring in his office when he should have been answering letters. Something in her spunk, I thought, might remind him of me as a younger girl.

"Not surprising," Priscilla said with a wry smile. "I think he's missed having someone to teach sword fighting."

"Agreed," I said, laughing.

Baxter trained his stare on me. "I've heard news around the loop and wanted to let you know."

My back tightened. Jikes, had Baxter already heard about my failed meeting with Matthias? The farther away I moved from that conversation, the more I wanted it to just stay in the past.

Way, way in the past.

"Oh?" I managed.

Baxter hesitated, no doubt drawing the suspense out on purpose, before he said, "Rumors of a demigod have surfaced not far from here. Presumed, anyway."

I couldn't help but wonder if it was the same as the one my father saw this morning.

"We haven't confirmed yet because witches are twitchy around anyone with a gem now," he continued, "but this rumor has substance. Mostly because the same gem has been reported in multiple places, but from different witches."

"What color is it?"

"Blue," he murmured. "Derek mentioned you saw a blue gem?"

I nodded, grateful to get the topic out of my head. If anyone would know whether this demigod was a problem, it was Baxter.

He let out a long breath. "It makes no sense, because a blue amulet would be a gem from Gelas. Gelas is a quiet, unobtrusive god. He has no reason to send his children here, and it's unlikely his children would rebel against him."

Gelas, god of ice, had little mention amongst discussions with Baxter. Likely because Gelas' children rarely did anything *to* merit discussion.

"Reports have seen mostly female, but occasionally a presumed male," Baxter murmured, speaking more to himself than us now. "Could be the same demigod just changing their appearance."

"And?" I asked. "Who could it be?"

Baxter shrugged. "Hard to tell. I don't know Gelas' children well. Ava has a few opinions on what demigods would be rummaging around here."

"Does she know which amulet it is?"

"Not for certain."

Ava, though only eleven, knew mortals back in Alaysia that made it their life's work to track amulets. The gods imbued powerful gems with magic and allowed their demigod children to use said magic. Mortals were unable to tolerate or use god magic, but children like Ava—half mortal, half demigod—sometimes had magical tolerance. They could be around it without pain, but not really access it.

The mortals that tracked the amulets and kept records had proven almost fanatical about it, with written charts, spies that reported magical use, and books dedicated to the different amulets.

Like an underground club of admirers that tracked everything.

"Presumably," I murmured, "*any* demigod might be interested in being here if there are magicless witches who can give allegiance to them and increase their power standing amongst the gods."

To that, Baxter said nothing.

Along with me, Papa, and a handful of others, Baxter lived in the camp that firmly believed that the demigods remained amongst us. The simple fact that life in Alkarra was easier than Alaysia, and natural curiosity on the demigod's part, would draw them closer. Not to mention the forbidden aspect of a new world. Apparently, the gods had forbidden travel to Alkarra for thousands of years.

I feared the truth was far uglier than that.

Baxter leaned back in his seat. His slumped posture allowed the full extent of his fatigue to show. He rarely let down his social guards to act like the rest of us. In my little cottage, though, he'd always found refuge.

"We still have a demigod situation to sort out," he murmured, eyes drawn low and contemplative. "News from my sister in Alaysia remains static. Said they heard that some of Ignis' sons are missing and might be associated with Bram, but no real clues yet."

"Meaning there is nothing they can do to help," Priscilla murmured.

Baxter nodded.

My fingers flexed into my palm involuntarily, driven by a shiver of heat that spread all the way to my bones. I tried to open my fingers one at a time, but they curled back in, as if my body wanted to conserve the god magic inside.

A dozen goddess-magic spells bubbled to the top of my mind, but I sent them away. Safer when I didn't toy with the powers while I felt the stirring god magic.

"I felt god magic the other day," I said. "In Chatham City when I visited Merrick. It was brief. Might have been something else but . . . I doubt it."

Baxter and I had many discussions about why I still felt flickers of heat in my body. Theories ranged from having some trapped inside me to a sensitivity to the use of goddess magic. Not all the theories made sense.

The sighting of the demigod with the blue barrette stirred new questions up in my mind.

The god magic *seemed* random, but what if it wasn't?

"That's not unusual for you, correct?" Baxter asked as he dragged a hand across his eyes. "If I remember right, you feel heat when you're in Chatham City fairly frequently."

"Yes."

"Do you feel it now?"

"Yes."

He frowned. "You also feel it consistently around me, no?"

I nodded. The thought had just occurred to me. Baxter and I didn't see each other much these days. Certainly not at my house.

"Perhaps you have god magic inside you that responds to being near amulets?" he suggested.

Logic dictated a strong likelihood that he was correct. "I hadn't thought of it, but I'd like to think that was the case," I murmured, mulling over the idea. "Certainly would make it easier to find the demigods if it were true."

He nodded, contemplative. "We'll figure it out."

As always, certainty filled his tone. Whether it was being the son of a god, a powerful demigod, or someone that had been reverentially adored by mortals for most of his life—which, now that I thought about it, I didn't know how long it had been—Baxter had a way of showing up in the world with something like arrogance. One couldn't call him arrogant or chauvinistic because he was too kind for that, but his confidence flirted with that line.

"The more pressing concern is, I think, your agreement with Prana to get rid of the demigods," he continued. "Any update or word from the goddess?"

I nearly groaned from the reminder. When I wasn't trying to convince other witches that the Sisterhood deserved a chance, I searched for demigods in an attempt to satisfy Prana. In exchange for my magic, I'd agreed to banish the demigods from Alkarra.

Fruitlessly.

"Not yet," I said. "She set no terms for my part of our bargain beyond banishing the demigods. Didn't threaten to take it back by a certain time, or anything."

"She's a goddess."

The words were issued as a warning. A reminder. Though Prana had formed an agreement with me and immediately fulfilled her end of the bargain, that didn't stop her from calling in my favor whenever she wanted. I had little doubt she saw or knew more than I presumed, but *how* the goddess operated, I didn't know.

What were her powers?

Her abilities?

Her motivations?

Prana's desperation had been real enough at the time, but that's all I knew. I sighed, burdened by the thought. Prana circled my head periodically, chased by the fear that I'd lose my magic all over again if I didn't get the demigods out.

"I'll go see Sanako tomorrow," I said, more to myself than him. Sanako, my friend from the West, was the perfect candidate to teach me more about Prana. "She knows more about goddesses than anyone else, presumably. I mean, she's a librarian at the Great Library of Burke and all . . . besides, I went searching for demigods yesterday and the day before, and found nothing. Again."

Baxter shared a sympathetic look. Most searching witches in Alkarra had the same, empty complaint. No one could find the demigods.

Except for Papa, apparently.

His gaze darted to Priscilla, then back to me in question. Priscilla had propped her chin in her hand and stared out at the forest, lost in thought. I regarded her with curiosity, realizing she hadn't spoken in quite awhile. Usually, she enjoyed when other witches came, which was extremely rare.

"She okay?" he mouthed.

I nodded.

"Can we talk outside?" he asked out loud this time.

Priscilla blinked out of her thoughts, saw Baxter gathering plates, and smiled sheepishly. "Sorry," she murmured with a little yawn.

"You didn't miss anything." I sent a spell to stack the dishes in the half-barrel where we washed them. They zipped out of Baxter's hands and over to the thin, long table where the barrel sat under a window. He sent me an annoyed eye roll.

"Witches," he muttered, "are too dependent on magic by half."

I grinned. "When I can be, I'm grateful to be. Priscilla, we're going to step outside to talk, all right?"

"Sure. Good to see you, Baxter."

She yawned again and peeled away from the table, toward the bed on the other side of a wooden partition. In the summer, I often slept outside. Now that snow and cold had come, I'd moved inside. To make room for Priscilla in the bed, I slept on the floor, near the fire. Baxter and I strolled by it as we headed out the main door.

He led me outside, then closed the door behind us. We advanced into the forest together, breath puffing ahead. Darkness had fallen, but my eyes adjusted to the shadows quickly.

"I have a question about Merrick," Baxter said.

I raised my eyebrow. A question about Papa made sense, or one about Ava, even. Swords, weapons, training, magic, those all came up in our conversations often enough. Merrick was one topic I'd never expected Baxter to surface.

"Oh?"

He frowned, clearly bothered by something. "He came to my office the other day with a question."

"A question from an Ambassador?" I mock-gasped. "Noteworthy, for sure."

Baxter lifted an eyebrow at my sarcasm and kept going. "He asked if I knew a demigod named Jote. He's the son of Ignis, god of fire."

I paused, brow lifted in a wordless question. Baxter stared beyond me now. His frown deepened.

"Jote is . . . trouble."

"So why would Merrick ask about him?"

"I don't know." He shook his head. "For Merrick being relatively new to politics, I was startled by his ability to avoid my questions. I'm not sure why he asked about Jote, but it can't be good, whatever it is."

A hundred possibilities spun through my mind, most of them enough to turn my blood cold.

"What makes Jote so bad?"

"He's a favorite of Ignis, and ruthless. He enjoys taunting, stalking, and hunting. To him, power is tantamount. If he has a goal, he pursues it with relentlessness. He enjoys the journey of bringing someone down more than the outcome, so he'll make it last. Anyway, I have an idea that Merrick is trying to find Jote. Do you know anything about it?"

"Not to that detail."

Concern lined his face. "You need to tell him to back off."

I pulled in a breath, thinking back to Farah's death. The silence Merrick maintained around this topic. Not to mention the "project" that he relentlessly pursued and the general frustration and uneasiness he often displayed. My brow wrinkled at the connecting dots.

"Baxter, is there any chance that demigods may have been meddling in Network affairs for a while now?" I asked, head tilted. "Before Bram, I mean?"

He paused, thinking that over. "I . . . suppose so. When your father interrogated him, Bram said he first came over before Mabel had become Almorran Master. He saw what could happen with witches if the Southern Network broke the Mansfeld Pact—as Mabel planned—and he started his bid for leadership then. It worked out in his favor."

"You have been kind and open and talented, but you were that way in Alaysia, according to Ava. But what if your father wasn't the only god with the same idea? To send a son or daughter to Alkarra to . . . see what was happening. Except, assume the reverse," I added. "Maybe Ignis or Tontes sent some of their children here to . . . make problems."

"If that's true," he murmured, "then it's troubling."

"Very."

A message appeared in front of Baxter with Papa's wax seal. He accepted it absently, still deep in thought.

"I don't know about Merrick and why he's talking about Jote," I said to turn the conversation back. "But I'll talk to him."

"Warn him," Baxter said, jaw tight. "If he needs to deal with Jote, it'd be best to involve me. A witch would be nothing but a toy to Jote, and if Merrick does have some kind of vendetta against him, he'd be a fool to try to pursue it. Let him know, all right?"

I nodded. "Thank you."

Baxter moved as if to leave, then stopped. From the flickering light inside, I could just make out curiosity in his features.

"Merrick is still interested in you, isn't he?"

My thoughts tied themselves into knots until I couldn't have formed a word if my life depended on it. Could it be said that Merrick still had a romantic interest in me? Yes, I thought so.

But . . . it *hadn't* been said. At least, not between Merrick and me.

Not officially.

Baxter made a sound in his throat. "I'd place currency on the bet that he is still romantically interested in you," he said firmly. "I'm curious what you think about that."

"I'm not sure."

"Give it some thought, then?"

"But . . . why?"

The muscles in his face softened, easing his intense expression. Baxter's hand lifted from his side, but stopped. He hesitated. I caught a glimpse of uncertainty. That side of him appeared so rarely that shock derailed my thoughts.

"He may not be the only interested party," Baxter

murmured, "and inquiring minds would like to know what you think of a romantic attachment."

The gentle hush of his words, accompanied by a boyish smile, made my heart twist. Before I could respond, Baxter drew in a deep breath. His arm dropped back to his side.

"Well, with that being said, I have a meeting with your father. A pentacle says that he's with Ava, teaching her how to fight again. The man has correspondences up to his ears and I found him sparring with Matthias this morning."

Matthias' name made my heart tighten in my throat. I managed a smile—pained as it must have appeared—and said, "Tell Papa I said merry meet."

"I will." Baxter winked. "See you soon, Bianca."

He strode into the forest, then disappeared several steps away.

Trust Baxter to be subtle, yet still confident. He hadn't said that *he* was the other interested party, but his body language and mannerisms indicated it all the same. A hundred different shades of confusion swirled through my mind.

Thinking about Baxter in that light turned my thoughts into wet cotton, so I turned back inside.

So much about *both* of those men didn't make sense.

The waves in the Western Network greeted me with a friendly *swish* as they rushed around my bare toes the next day. Their foamy fingers slipped back, then surged forward again as if they couldn't stay away.

I closed my eyes and drew in a deep breath of wet, salty air. A band of humidity lay across the distant ocean, lost to the sapphire edge of the sky. Not far away, a fishing vessel rocked on the calm waves, sail unfurled.

The tang of sea breeze on the back of my throat sent a

shiver of joy all the way through my muscles. I should have brought Priscilla with me. She would have enjoyed this taste of ocean and sky again. Questions of demigods, magicks, Baxter, and Merrick shuffled to the side in the wild air.

I breathed the openness in deeply.

Only the sea provided such a wide, barren expanse. An odd juxtaposition. Underneath, the waters teemed with life. Above the deep ocean currents, the sea demanded sacrifices of witch and mortal and sky, feeding all it obtained to Prana's lower kingdoms. She swept life away in water, wind, and terror, harboring a vast, strange world even more frightening than Letum Wood's closed canopy.

A shout to my left drew my attention.

Two small children scampered toward me. Behind them, an older girl around my age followed. Her dark, silky hair trailed behind her in the breeze. A monocle hung from a chain near her neck, bouncing as she strode through the sand. In the distance behind the approaching party, several sprawling huts populated the beach. They'd been pinched together from collected driftwood, braids of sinewy grasses that shivered nearby, and generations of love.

Sanako, Librarian over the historical folktales in the Division of God and Goddess History at the Great Library of Burke, smiled as she approached.

Her two younger brothers ran ahead of her, joy at my arrival written all over their faces. They jumped, attempting to wrestle me into the sand. I laughed, fought them off, and sent a spell to lift them into the air. They giggled, flailing arms and legs, until I set them carefully back down.

Several attempts to send me into the air with a spell met with failure, so I defeated them with a spell that kicked sand up from the ground and skittered in a whirl around them. They laughed, spinning with it.

The toothy twins with bare chests and bright brown eyes

laughed as they shook sand from their straight black hair and sprinted back into the waves, where they always played. Sanako reached me then, a book tucked under one arm. She lifted two fingers in a Western Network greeting.

"Merry meet, Bianca!"

"Merry meet, Sanako."

She gazed after her brothers and shook her head. "They're wild," she muttered. "Tried to swim out after a sea dragon the other day. Said they wanted to ride it."

I grinned. "Sounds like fun."

Sanako eyed me, her gaze dropping to my calves. "I didn't know you were coming today. Something wrong with your boots?"

"No, not at all."

Relief showed in her relaxing posture. "Good," she murmured. "The strengthening spells on the laces are new, but the magic hasn't failed us yet. Baba's work with the grimoire has been paying off."

Although Sanako made currency with her work at the Great Library of Burke, her extended family had more witches than her salary alone could support. Forty witches and four generations lived together in their beachside huts, and they all supported one another. Her father—or Baba—ran a sandal business that I loved, but it hadn't kept up with the unstable economy after the war, even with all the business I'd sent their way.

Currency was a painful discussion everywhere.

"You want to speak with me outside the Great Library of Burke, I presume?" she asked next, suspicion thick in her voice. "It's been a while."

My expression sobered. "Yes. I have questions about Prana. It's a conversation that's long overdue, I think."

An understanding expression followed. "Ah, yes. Rumors say you received your magic back."

I paused, then nodded. Papa, Leda, Scarlett, the Central Network leadership, and handfuls of other discreet witches knew I'd received my magic back—and how—but the return of my magic had been a discussion point we hadn't yet explained to the world. It was one of the few points the Council and I had agreed upon when we cleaned up the mess after the Celebration.

How did Sanako know? Most witches had gone back to their own lives, and I lived quietly in the forest. The moment witches in the Networks and outside my regular circles knew I somehow lost my magic and had it restored, things in the Southern Network could explode. Magicless witches would hunt me down to beg for their own cure, or flood Letum Wood or take unnecessarily to the sea.

For now, it seemed best to live in my trees and let the world unfold.

Curiosity filled her expression, which had always been happy, if not a bit distracted by other thoughts. Right now, I saw focus and concentration. She tilted her head to the side, away from the beach.

"Follow me, I know a spot."

* * *

Sanako led me farther back, where vague grasses grew taller than me. They scraped under my knees, the tips sharp as thorns. Sanako didn't seem to notice their stabbing influence when she plopped into them, crossed-legged, sitting there as if she did this every day.

"I'm ready," she declared.

I gazed around. Not another soul in sight. Just the mournful sound of a gentle breeze off the sea. Another thorn scratched my skin and I winced.

"Ouch. Oh . . . this is . . . great. No one will bother us

here," I added softly, shoving aside another piece of grass before it gouged my thigh.

She stifled a laugh. "These grasses are natural deterrents for my brothers. They may seem carefree and innocent, but they're the greatest spies my old baba—my grandfather in your terms—has ever had. My brothers act oblivious, but they listen to everything. Witches underestimate children's intelligence all the time."

She said the last sentence like a warning, and I took it as such. Indeed, I never would have presumed they'd spy or report to anyone. They seemed too carefree for something so adult, but I couldn't deny that they would make compelling spies. My thoughts flittered to Ava. Perhaps she could be—or do—the same. I reined that thought back in to focus on the matter at hand.

"I need your help, Sanako."

"You met Prana," she said promptly. "She also probably made you a deal that forced you to do something unpleasant that she's trying to avoid in exchange for your magic."

My jaw dropped.

"How did you know?"

Her lips twitched. "Your magic has been fully restored, Bianca. Rumors abound everywhere, though I doubted their veracity until I heard one that said you met a goddess. Now *that* rumor made sense."

She shrugged.

"Why didn't you contact me?" I asked.

She shrugged again, more dramatically this time. "What was there to say? It all made sense! I figured it was Prana because the only goddess that would reveal herself is one that needs something. Desperately, so. Deasylva historically worked by more subtle means. She also has the least amount of energy because she pushes so much of her attention into Letum Wood. She's also the least likely to get herself into a desperate situation. Selsay, the goddess of mountains, wouldn't want anything to do with you . . ."

She prattled into the background of my thoughts for a minute, and I scrambled to keep up with her. Goddess names and facts slipped off her lips, as easily as if these deities were her friends.

Only a few months ago, Sanako had boasted that she thought she met a goddess. She hadn't been sure—had vaguely mentioned something about queer eyes. Prana's eyes had been queer, all right.

I cleared my throat, shook off my surprise, and said, "I suppose you'd be the one to know the most about what a goddess would or wouldn't do. Right now, I need a little help understanding Prana."

She grinned, revealing slightly crooked front teeth. The smile quickly faded into something far more serious, like the Sanako I knew from the library.

"Tell me everything and leave out no details," she said. "When it comes to Prana, the smallest thing makes the biggest difference."

"But—"

"I'll explain more when you're done."

I wanted to ask her how she could *possibly* know with any certainty, but who was I to ask? Sanako knew more about goddesses than any witch in Alkarra and stood as my best bet. Before I could voice my doubt, Sanako wrapped her arms around her knees and stared out at the ocean.

Families in this part of the Western Network took offense at eye contact during intense stories or emotional exchanges. Leda had explained it when I realized Sanako rarely held my gaze if I asked how her family was doing. I wondered if I frightened her somehow.

"You may begin," Sanako said.

With a nod, I complied. I told her every detail that I could recall, starting with how I lost my magic when I touched an amulet forged by the god of fire, Ignis. How the touch left my insides smoldering like coal and fire and ash, and created an empty chasm in my soul without magic. Then the day in Letum Wood weeks later, when I'd started to resign myself to the thought of being a witch without magic. Water had appeared on the ground and led me to a garden where Prana revealed herself.

"She wanted me to guarantee that I'd banish the demigods from Alkarra if she gave me my magic back," I finished with a shrug. "She returned it right then. It felt . . . strange for days. Like she'd overfilled me, or something. Eventually, that's gone away. Now I just . . . I hum."

Sanako's gaze snapped over to mine. "Did you agree to banish the demigods?"

"Ah . . . yes?"

"Bianca!" she cried. "What were you thinking?"

Her reprimand cut deep. I winced, entirely aware that taking the deal from a goddess may not have been my wisest decision, but Prana hadn't given me time to debate my options out.

"I was thinking that I wanted my magic back."

She opened her mouth to say something else, then closed it again. Her fingers opened and then curled shut over and over again. Her silence sent a foreboding feeling through me. At that moment, Prana's demands had seemed easy enough. The entire force of Alkarra had been determined to banish the demigods.

But now we couldn't find any . . .

"I . . . I had to take it, Sanako," I murmured. "You can't imagine what it's like to lose your magic. It feels like losing . . . everything."

Sanako swallowed. "It's just . . . of all the goddesses to make a bargain with?" She swallowed, hair swaying around her neck as she shook her head. Her tone dropped. "She's the worst. Prana probably created this demigod mess in the first place. She's using you to save herself in front of her sisters, I'd wager."

"I never thought she was trying to be charitable," I muttered. "Look, can you tell me more about Prana? I don't know when she's going to call my deal in. I don't know what to expect."

"Death, probably," Sanako snapped. "If you don't fulfill your end of the bargain, she'll kill you."

"Great," I whispered.

Sanako frowned. "Prana is . . . devious and quickly bored. I don't know what has happened here to cause her to enlist the help of a witch. You said that she mentioned Sanna Spence while telling you about it?"

"Yes."

"Then that means . . . *something*."

"Something bad?"

"Probably. Probably something terrible." Sanako shuddered. "Prana likes to create complicated magical systems, then abandon them. The magic of the Dragonmasters? That was Prana. She created the races of dragons and allowed her sisters to adopt the magic to their own effect, but she also enslaved those dragons. Instead of creating the magic in a way that freed the dragons, she let it exist as a system of slavery. Eventually, Sanna destroyed it through a loophole that not even Prana anticipated. Prana's the only goddess that doesn't finish things and the one that stirs up the most trouble."

Her ominous words fell like gongs inside my head. Was magic worth whatever Prana might bring my way?

Yes.

Every day.

Which meant I just had to fix this problem before it became a *true* disaster. "What do I do?" I asked.

"You banish the demigods," she muttered.

I snorted. A thousand thoughts swirled up with her statement. The Sisterhood. The demigod that Papa and I independently spotted near Chatham City on two different occasions. Prana's strange gaze when she peered at me, presumably into my soul.

"I'm already trying to find the demigods. It's my main plan and I make steps toward it every day . . . but it's not happening as quickly as I wanted. I'm afraid that she's going to pop up at any time and take the magic."

"Prana likely wants this disaster to end. If she thinks you're her best bet, she's probably watching. If she hasn't interfered by now, then I'd say keep doing what you're doing."

To my surprise, her words gave me some comfort.

"Thanks."

A shuffle of wind stirred the grasses around our ankles, whistling softly. The hollow tops of the grasses bounced in the breeze and carried a lonely sound, interrupted only by the occasional giggle of her brothers in the surf.

A furrowed look of concentration stole over her profile. "Did the god magic go away?" she asked.

"I don't think so."

"For some reason," she muttered in annoyance, "the history scrolls don't cover the deeper intricacies of magic."

Whether it was the ridiculousness of this conversation, or a need for release, both of us broke into giggles. Releasing something besides stress felt nice, and I let the laugh trail into the wind.

"I'm trying to start a Sisterhood of Protectors," I said, "and use it to banish the demigods. I will meet with the Central Network Council tomorrow to see if I can get their approval for funding and training."

"I heard."

"About the Sisterhood?"

Sanako flipped her hand. "Yes, but just rumors. Old baba pays to remain *very* well-informed, remember?" She tapped the side of her head, then pointed to her brothers. "They spy well, the imps."

"What do these rumors say?"

"Nothing of importance," she said quickly, without looking my way.

My cheeks flared with heat. They were jokes, then. Witches making fun of my attempt to re-create the Brotherhood in a Network that didn't even allow women to be Guardians. I skipped several decades of common sense and dove right to the meat of what the Network needed. Most witches wouldn't like that.

"Using the Sisterhood to banish the demigods would serve two main purposes: prove the value of a Sisterhood and fulfill my deal with Prana. I just . . . I'm not sure how to do it because there's so much about Prana I don't know. And I haven't found any demigods."

Sanako seemed to mull that over, and the lonely whine of the breeze rang in the background. She turned to me, gazing at me for the first time since we settled into this bed of sharp reeds.

"I've already told you most of what I know about Prana. I'll see if I can find a way to locate more. Prana has probably done something stupid and seeks to rectify it before her sisters punish her. At least, history tells us that has happened before."

"Can one goddess do that to another goddess?"

She shrugged. "Let's hope so. The next best thing that I can say is to watch your back. Prana sounds desperate, and witches don't matter to her. If she comes back? Say nothing without me there. Send for me with a scroll that has the words *she returns* and I'll immediately follow the magic back to you. Understand?"

"Yes. Thank you."

Sanako stood, brushing old grass off her legs. The slapping sound of her hand against fabric made a dull thud. I stood next to her, grateful to get out of the sharp daggers.

"If there is one goddess I would have cautioned you against trusting, it's Prana," Sanako said with a resigned sigh. "Stay away from water and banish the demigods. That's the best advice that I can give."

Chapter Four

My stomach twisted as I stared at Papa's apartment door and tried to gather my courage.

Somewhere in the background, Reeves puttered around with a duster, swiping invisible specks off of things that had already been cleaned. His gentle ministrations soothed me.

Moments later, Reeves appeared behind me, using his fingers to brush my shoulders off and straighten my dress.

"Thank you," I said wryly.

He bustled off.

While I waited for seven more minutes to pass before Council Member Greyson's Assistant would come to escort me into the Esbat, I started to pace. Sitting down could wrinkle my dress, a simple, gray piece with a low waist, long sleeves, conservative skirts all the way to the floor, and boots lined with soft, white rabbit fur. Movement felt better anyway.

The Sisterhood is an opportunity to better our defenses against future foes.

We can work together with the Council and the Brotherhood.

The definition of terms are as follows . . .

Leda and I had stayed up until past midnight to cement the phrases I'd use, the tone in which I'd deliver them, and how to hold my shoulders. The diplomacy effort nearly broke my brain. So much propriety for propriety's sake never made sense to me. I forced myself to focus and concentrate.

The Sisterhood deserved this shot.

A scroll popped into the air in front of me. I blinked, then tapped the edge. The note unfurled, filled with a familiar, scratchy handwriting.

Good luck today, B. You can do this.

—M

My heart fluttered a little. Merrick. How kind of him to remember. Baxter's cryptic observation of Merrick's habits and questions from several nights before ran back through my head, but I pushed them away for another day. I'd talk to Merrick tomorrow, when I filled him in on what happened at the Esbat.

A light *tap tap tap* on the door brought Reeves to it in seconds. He cast me a questioning look. I nodded. With a quick scan of my outfit and an approving nod, he twisted the door knob, gazed outside, then opened it wider.

"Your escort, Miss Bianca," he murmured.

A quiet, pleasant-looking witch waited outside. She wore a maroon dress and a scarf around dark hair. She nodded to me, then to Reeves, and gestured with a hand into the hallway.

"Please," she murmured, "come with me."

Thankfully, she didn't make small talk as we headed toward the Council room. I certainly didn't need an escort, but the Council loved control and routine. I gave way to their traditions in the hope that it built trust.

My nerves had properly frayed by the time the Assistant tugged the Council doors open and motioned me inside. It felt like a novelty to stroll in with an Assistant instead of sneak inside.

A large table swamped with chairs. Fifteen or so witches littered the room in varying stages of sitting or standing. Assistants fluttered around the edges, where quills and ink pots and parchments hovered in the air, furiously taking notes. The general bustle lent a harried feeling.

Several pairs of eyes turned to us as we entered. Upon seeing me, most of them darkened considerably. I ignored the obvious displeasure of several Council Members and locked my gaze on one.

Greyson, the representative from the Western Covens.

He had alacrity and neutrality in spades, and he'd be my only hope for a successful meeting here. Although I didn't want to admit it, the prospect of the Sisterhood lived or died on the support it received from the Council. Although Council Members loyal to my father were still here, that meant nothing for my hope to inspire a Sisterhood.

In this regard, I stood alone.

General murmurs of conversation increased in volume as the Assistant led me further into the room. The doors closed behind us, and a burst of light from the corner of my eyes indicated that a silencing incantation prevented listening ears from the outside.

"We need something to *hold* the demigods," said a crackly old voice on the right side of the table. "They're naturally stronger than us. How in the name of the good gods can any Protector or Guardian waylay a demigod, hold them, and not have their nose or arm broken? Baxter proved that most demigods could break our manacles. We don't have metal strong enough for the job."

The blustering voice came from Halifax, a wheezy man from the Southern Covens who had been a Council Member for the last fifteen years. He had a deep, abiding loyalty to my father, but an irascibility that tarnished his more positive traits. I, for one, appreciated his straightforwardness.

Most didn't.

He spoke with Aldred, the man who led the opposition against my father. Aldred was a portly man, with a prominent belly and matching arrogance. Leda didn't think highly of him, but her opinion lay solely on a lack of political savviness and flexibilty. Mine weighed heavily on personal dislike.

Aldred's nose wrinkled as I stopped a few paces away from the Council table. All of the Council Members turned to face me, so I forced a serene expression. On purpose, I didn't allow my gaze to linger on Greyson for more than a moment.

"Issue number fourteen," squeaked a woman named Martha. "The presentation of a defensive idea from Bianca Monroe."

Martha sat on my right. She was a middle-aged woman with curls like mole burrows all over her head. She could slip a pencil in one side and out the other across her scalp. The curls glimmered in tones of auburn and gray as she consulted a parchment that had been criss-crossed with ink and notes all over it. The tattered thing looked ready to fall apart.

She blinked behind her glasses, then peered up at me with pinched lips. "A defensive idea?" she murmured. "Now what does that mean?"

"Yes," Aldred called from across the way. "What *must* the infamous Bianca Monroe have to say this time? You have four-and-a-half minutes left."

His long-suffering tone rankled me, but I ignored him.

Instead, I fell into the memorized grooves that Leda and I had practiced all night, grateful to have a place to land.

"Council, thank you for the honor of being able to stand before you—"

"You're wasting our time with platitudes," Aldred muttered.

I pinched my lips and swallowed hard.

"To the heart of the matter," I said, skipping two other memorized lines. "I would like to present to you the idea of a Sisterhood of Protectors."

My gaze roved the table, soaking in their initial reactions. Several of Papa's supporters didn't flinch. Somehow, they already knew, I'd wager. Had likely heard rumors. From Matthias? Scarlett, perhaps? If Sanako's old baba heard rumblings, *someone* had been talking about it.

Aldred's followers displayed widened eyes. Raised eyebrows. Shocked whispers. One older woman named Rosanna leaned back, mouth open. "A Sisterhood?" she cried. "What does that even mean?"

"Thank you for asking," I quickly said. These were Leda's words, not mine, and they felt stiff on my tongue. "Allow me to explain. For as long as recorded history, we've had various forms of a Brotherhood of Protectors. Although the organization went by different names—"

"We don't have questions about the Brotherhood," Rosanna replied. "You have less than four minutes left to tell us your idea."

My heart thumped, rankled at the Sisterhood being demoted to an *idea*. The Sisterhood had become my entire life. Forced to swallow my reaction, I had no choice. No more Leda. No more propriety.

Time for Bianca.

I abandoned the pretense by leaning forward, planting my hands on the table, and staring right at Aldred.

"I want to start a Sisterhood of Protectors that mimics what the Brotherhood does, only with women. Ten women who show exceptional discipline, love of Network, and talent with magic. We'll train and work with the Brotherhood to keep the Network safe."

"Do you think so little of our Protectors now?" Aldred asked.

"No." I lifted my chin. "There's no one in this room that knows the Brotherhood as well as me, nor holds as much respect. I've sacrificed time, relationships, and more to the Brotherhood just like they have."

I spared several moments to gaze around, but no one challenged me. With a breath, I straightened, removing my hands from the table. I set them on the back of a chair and met the eyes of other Council Members present.

"Women should have a place everywhere, even in a defense of our Network. We have strengths that men don't have. We can get into places where it might be difficult for the Brotherhood to access. Methods that—"

"An insult," huffed Xander, a lean witch who reminded me of an empty glass bottle. Hollow, thin, and ready to topple at the next burst of wind. His enlarged mustache grew over an upper lip that disappeared in the brown bristles. "And a distraction," he added quickly, flipping a hand. "A Sisterhood would be a novelty, not a reality, and during a time when we don't have novelty to spare."

Greyson stood from his chair on the other side of the table. His calm eyes collided with mine.

"What did you come here for, Bianca?" he asked quietly. "What do you want from your Council to enact this idea?"

"Approval and funding."

Several scowls formed at this.

"Until I can promise training and wages to interested women, I don't have an organization. I won't waste their time or Network resources. I came to the Council to ask for good-faith funding, use of the Protector's training equipment, and leadership resources to get us started."

"What does *leadership resources* mean?" another witch asked. I didn't know his name, but he blinked every five seconds and yawned every other minute.

"Access to trainers," I said. "Marten, maybe. Matthias. Anyone who could help us learn and improve."

"Can you imagine the budget that would require?" Aldred said to the room at large, then tsked under his breath. He reached for his pipe with a dismissive turn of his back. I wanted to wrap my fingers around his neck and shake as hard as I could.

"Do you feel this is a good time for the Sisterhood?" Greyson asked. "With issues rising from the demigod question, it seems that diverting resources from the Brotherhood might be a mistake."

"Unless divergent resources had similar results, if not better," I pointed out, grateful for the lobby of a good question. "It depends on how you look at it. A Brotherhood *and* a Sisterhood could work well together against our current threats. The foremost of which is the demigods, of course. Fortunately, the demigod problem is quite simple, really."

The room quieted at once.

I blinked, startled at the unexpected lack of sound. Aldred turned and straightened out of his chair again, his face intent.

"Pardon me," he murmured. "Did you say the demigod situation is simple?"

"Yes."

Astonished faces blinked at me.

"While largely unknown," I continued, "the demigods are extremely limited by one weakness: their amulets. If you want to subdue a demigod, you get the amulet. Without it, they're nothing but a mortal with greater strength and charisma. That's it."

Several beats of calm passed before several witches began to speak at once. Amidst the garbled words, phrases stuck out.

"Not that simple."

"Simple doesn't mean it's an easy fix."

"We don't know what's an amulet and what isn't!"

"Want witches to lose their magic trying, do you?"

"Shame on you."

Dread pooled in my belly. This had gone wildly out of hand.

"Wait, please," I called. "All I meant is that our greatest problem isn't overcoming their magic. Our greatest problem is finding them. Once we know their location, managing the demigods becomes a simple fact of getting the amulets."

Halifax tilted his head, gaze tapered. Even Greyson appeared to be in deeper thought, though his expression gave little away. The rest increased their uproar. The frantic energy of the room rose with each exclamation of annoyance from them.

"The demigods are gone," said a droll voice. A black-haired man with a riotous beard that dropped halfway to his navel rapped on the table with meaty knuckles. "Our education initiatives in the Southern Network have sent them back to their land. They aren't here."

A few murmurs of agreement rose behind him. "It's been months," Aldred replied to another Council Member—though not very quietly. "They would have come back by now if they were here at all."

"That's shortsighted rubbish."

The words escaped me before I could pull them back. Based on the outraged expressions of various Council Members, I already knew I'd lost the battle.

"You haven't lost your magic," I cried, "so you don't

comprehend the price of what you could lose if the demigods are still here. Dismissing the demigods because of an education initiative is . . . insane. There are still witches desperate to get their magic back. *Any* magic back, no matter the costs. Regardless of your education initiative, if a demigod offers them magic, they will take it."

"At the price of their freedom?" Greyson asked.

"Yes! It's a situation that I have intimate knowledge of. The desperation for any magic is . . . powerful. Overwhelming. If a demigod offers these witches something *like* magic . . ."

I let it trail away.

Their troubled expressions grew long, the silence damning.

Martha stood up, drawing all eyes. She eyed me with disdain. "It's regrettable what happened to you, but let's not forget you have your magic back. Shall we return to the point?" She turned to the room at large. "Her time has long since passed. Matthias informed me that Bianca has already asked him about the Sisterhood."

She sent me a droll look, her high-pitched voice a grating irritant to the ears. The bottom fell out of my stomach.

Oh, no.

"He's already told her he feels it's a distraction," Martha continued. "She comes to us without outside support in a last-ditch effort to find a way to be paid to play with weapons. Entitlement, that's all this is. Not to mention she made a deal with a goddess to get her magic back and she needs to fulfill it. She's using Network funding to find the demigods, something she agreed to, independent from us. Additional point: Bianca Monroe is as wild as they come to this day, and she would not make a proper leader."

Fury boiled in me at Martha's insinuation, Matthias's betrayal, and the heady assumptions she based her opinion on. I breathed through it, calling back on the training that Papa had given me years ago. The same training that drove me to the Sisterhood.

The same training that would one day save their lives.

"What about Scarlett?" Aldred asked me. "What has she said about it? I'm sure you've floated this to her."

"Scarlett has no opinion on the Sisterhood," I replied, then added to my final detriment, but her political safety, "She's too busy with her responsibilities as High Priestess to help me with leadership support."

Aldred laughed, a sound so gleeful it could have been a giggle. "You see?" He pointed to me. "Not even the High Priestess, a known sympathizer to this wild girl, will support her efforts. This has been a waste of our time and I call for the motion to end."

A fist on the table punctuated his cry.

"She's also harboring the Eastern Network mistress," another witch called. "What's her name?"

"Priscilla," called another.

"Spy for the Eastern crown in our midst, you think?" Aldred scoffed and leaned back, frowning so deeply his lips compressed into fat lines. "And this girl wants more power in our Network? As if her father didn't spoil her enough."

Others glared more deeply.

Several voices exploded in agreement, echoing through the chamber. What little support amongst Papa's loyal Council Members evaporated like dust in the wind. Amidst the chaos, Aldred smiled at me like a lecherous snake, then prodded a few more Council Members to fury. The mess continued. Only Greyson peered at me, something like concern, perhaps curiosity, in the straight lines of his face.

"Get her out of here!" Aldred waved at me the way one would swat away a pest. "We have *real* matters to discuss."

Greyson's Assistant stepped forward. "Come," she whispered, barely audible over the rising din. Hopes dashed, I turned to follow her out the doors. Before they closed, I glanced back to see the chaos at the table growing two-fold. Aldred saluted me with a jaunty grin.

The doors thudded closed behind me.

* * *

Baxter waited for me at the cottage.

Priscilla was visiting Michelle, so my retreat home had been intentional. The joke of a meeting left me so riled up I couldn't even run. I just transported away in utter disbelief, then looked up to see Baxter waiting by my hearth.

"I saw the whole thing," he said.

Grateful to have someone there, I closed my door, leaned against it, and let out a long breath. Already, weariness began to replace the rage. The false accusations. The animosity. The sheer lack of respect for the idea.

How had Papa managed to work with them for so long?

"How?" I asked, swallowing my frustration back.

He quirked an eyebrow.

I sighed. "Right. God magic. They can't really detect it. That is . . . sort of unsettling."

"Should be extremely unsettling." He motioned to the table. "Sit. Let's talk. For the record, god magic is not a power that I wield often but . . . I wanted to see what happened when you presented your idea."

Grateful to have someone else's view on it, I obeyed his directive to sit, but only because I wanted something firm beneath me.

Baxter sat across the table, concern in his lovely, pale green eyes. Settling my body in a safe place felt like the first real time I'd drawn a full breath in hours.

Baxter placed his forearms on the table and leaned into them. A curl bounced on his forehead.

"First of all," a finger ticked in the air, "they never gave you a chance. There wasn't a single scenario in which you could have walked into that room today and gotten what you wanted. We could probably have Hiddleston go into the paths of the past to confirm my suspicion, if you wanted. Might make you feel better."

Uncomfortable with the truth, I dropped my gaze. Despite what he said, I felt all the way to my bones that he was right. Maybe I'd known before I went there. Maybe I'd sensed that Council support would never happen.

"No," I murmured. "I don't need Hiddleston to confirm it. Maybe the only reason I was even allowed to appear is that most of them hadn't looked at the list of issues being presented."

"Agreed. And . . ." he hesitated, then continued, "that's my fault, actually. I intentionally caused a delay with the agenda so they couldn't see who was coming today. Only Greyson reviewed the full lineup and he received it one minute before the official start of the meeting." Baxter's lips twitched. "Let's just say that it worked in your favor."

For a moment, I could only stare at him. Was I relieved or annoyed that he'd worked behind-the-scenes to make this happen? Maybe a little of both. Amused, if anything, that he admitted it so sheepishly.

With a wry smile I said, "Thanks. I think."

He shrugged, then leaned forward until his heavy hand dropped on top of mine. It felt soft and firm. A surprising comfort.

"I'm sorry, B," he said with a tired sigh. "It's clear that the Council won't support you. They were unnecessarily accusative, harsh, and caustic, but even if they'd been polite, they were never going to give you what you wanted. Despite all of that, it was something you needed to do. You gave them the opportunity to support you, and they didn't take it. Now, you'll figure out a path. I know you will."

My nostrils flared as I took that in. Then I leaned back because he felt too close. Everything felt too close, and I realized too late that I should have run. Should have taken off into the forest until my chest hurt, just like I did after Matthias's conversation.

"The world doesn't want this Sisterhood to happen. It's like I keep hitting walls everywhere I turn."

"Walls don't matter," Baxter said quietly. "You're looking for a crack, a window, a door."

My brow furrowed. True. Perhaps I'd asked too much of the Council today. Played too many cards in hope of getting an easy path forward. In truth, there was no easy way to create the Sisterhood. I would have to circumvent tradition, create a new culture, and bring women into a position of power in a new way.

"I haven't given up," I said, responding to a silent question that hummed between us. Hints of relief appeared in Baxter's gaze. "I just . . . I realize now that I need to switch my strategy."

Baxter's gaze gleamed with sudden light.

"Or," he murmured, "work the advantages that you have. The Council may not have been respectful or receptive tonight, but one witch was asking the right questions."

"Greyson."

"Greyson," he repeated. "I have little doubt Scarlett's been hedging her bets with him. Perhaps sharing information, preparing him for this day? Maybe not, but I wouldn't be surprised if she's tried to silently build up support for you in her own subtle way. He may be the crack in the Council wall that you need."

Greyson was new, young, yet still respected on the Council. His penchant for logic and facts over emotion and arguments made him something of a rarity. Because of Greyson, things were actually completed. He moved meetings forward, took everything seriously, and had the unique ability to look at things from varying angles before he made a decision.

He rolled through my mind now like a loose stone. Greyson had been the only one actually interested in what I had to say, and my opinions on the issue of the demigods seemed to pique his curiosity. Blinking, I looked at Baxter in surprise. A slow grin crossed his face.

"You understand?" he asked.

"Yes," I whispered. "It wasn't a total loss, was it? Infuriating, but not wasted. I had Greyson's attention."

Baxter slapped the top of the table. "Exactly. You had Greyson's attention, and maybe that's all you need. It may not be everything, but it's something. If I were you, I'd chase Greyson down for a one-on-one meeting and get *his* thoughts on it. That is your next step."

Plans sprouted through my mind, spinning together slowly, steadily. Greyson shouldn't be too hard to request an audience with, nor prepare to speak with. Although Leda had been helpful in preparing for the Council, I could do this one on my own.

Baxter leaned back, obviously satisfied with my response. "You understand it," he said. "Now, get to work."

He stood and headed toward the door. Halfway there he stopped, looked back, and said, "You represented yourself like the leader of the Sisterhood today, by the way. Your father would have been proud."

With that, he disappeared out the door.

Chapter Five

Early the next morning, I snuck through Letum Wood.

The bushes and undergrowth sensed me coming, visible or not, and bent out of the way as I crept by. Each footfall was intentionally placed, quiet, and rolled to avoid the snap of sound. Moving like this in the forest required ageless patience.

Today, I had it.

Keep your weight centered, Papa's voice whispered from my memories. *Find your focus and keep it. Sound has more power than you think. So does smell. Keep your other senses open.*

For that breath of time when I heard his voice in my head, I became a little girl again. Hungry to learn. Ready for more. Certain I held ability and power and the world at my feet. At the time, I had crept through Letum Wood, attempting to come up behind an animal without frightening them away.

Stealth, Papa had always said, *is second only to silence.*

These lessons looped silently through the back of my mind as I shuffled from one tree to another. The process was arduously slow, but through it I remained undetected. My only goal, really.

A thousand other things waited for my attention right now. More demigod searching, for one. We *needed* to find those demigods. My firewood pile, for another. Not to mention that I hadn't seen Ava in over a week. Merrick and I needed to have a chat about his ambitions with a certain demigod, apparently.

Yet, I ignored all of those things.

Once hidden, I pressed my spine to the trunk of a tree and listened. No change in noise or cadence. No pause that indicated all the witches whom I stalked had noticed me.

With the tips of my fingers, I touched my face. Charcoal came away, gritty and loose. Wasn't an ideal way to disguise myself, but shadows were better than skin tone in the forest. Anything that *wasn't* magic gave me an advantage against this group of warriors.

Know your target, Papa said in one final, fading whisper.

With a deep breath, I turned, assessed my targets, and crept forward to another tree. This time, the tree was hidden by shadow, which made my job a lot easier. Through the bracken, ten men were just visible.

"Another!" called a voice.

Sneaking up on Protectors as they trained in the forest was no easy task. Any regular witch would do it from above. Harder to track and less certainty there, with more escape routes in the trees. Protectors could transport up into the branches, of course, but landing on a branch a couple of paces across and not falling to your death was harder than a firm place on the ground.

The Protectors knew all of that, so they glanced that way often, twice as much as they looked around the forest floor. In certain situations, they would put incantations above them to catch potential meddling witches. Invisible nets. Bubbles which, once touched, burst with a terrific sound so a meddler could be located immediately.

The probability of anyone creeping up on them on foot was low, however, because they'd be able to respond so quickly. Based on my study, I could already tell the Protectors hadn't put as much observational power into what might be moving on the ground.

Not yet.

When I could discern individual facial features, but not eye color, I stopped. They'd be able to sense my magic in use from this distance, which is why I didn't use any. Instead, I wore a pair of slacks I'd filched from the fireboys' clean laundry stacks in the castle, with a white shirt I'd streaked with spots of dirt and charcoal, to mimic the local environment of snow on the dark earth. My hair was pulled into a low, tight bun so it was out of my face. Only the whites of my eyes would show against the black grit.

Pressed to the ground, bushes dropped over me as if I'd asked them to. The forest had always been able to read my thoughts, or perhaps discern my intentions. It helped me today, as it would forever.

Silent, I watched the Protectors through the cold bracken. Chill pressed into my stomach, the cold ground radiating through my thin clothes. I would have shivered, but I forced myself to hold still.

"Again," Matthias demanded.

Eight Protectors formed a circle around two in the middle. A short, stocky man with a bulldog-like expression was pitted against a witch that resembled a bear. Shaggy red hair, beard, and an upper body so thick it looked like a keg. The two collided in a physical brawl, slamming into each other in the middle of the circle. The remaining eight men watched with calculating gazes as the two grappled.

The brute strength of one pitted up against the other was

a daunting thing to witness. Rippling muscles and sheer ferocity propelled them back and forth. Despite the Protectors' unparalleled ability to do magic, Matthias often had them train without spells.

"If you can fight without magic," he often said, "then you can fight with it. Better to be prepared for the worst possible scenario."

Losing the ability to do magic was the worst possible scenario.

And none of them had lived through it.

Despite being a day behind me, the aftermath of the Council meeting lingered like a weight. After speaking to Baxter, I'd lain awake in bed, staring at the ceiling, thinking of Viveet. Why I thought of my old sword—who lay in tatters in the forest, hidden beneath a sapling—I didn't know. I couldn't get her out of my head.

Maybe because I didn't want to do this without her.

The two bullish-looking men peeled apart, the shorter of the two the champion for the round. Matthias had one thing right: without magic, no female would be able to take on their sheer brawn. The power behind their physically-different bodies proved a significant barrier. One I'd, perhaps, down-played because I didn't know how to change it. Did their powerful bodies negate my ability to run a Sisterhood?

Was sheer brawn really all it required?

No. Matthias of all witches should understand that. He had them train without magic so they were ready, but the Protector's ability to do magic, read a situation, and give their entire concentration over to a task is what set them apart from other witches.

"Rognvald," Matthias called. "Jermaine."

Two other men stepped forward into the circle. The others faded back, filling the empty slots. The shorter man who'd won had a bloody nose. The broader witch sported a bubbling bruise under one eye. Still, they grinned, looking triumphant.

Physical advantage, indeed.

I inched backward slowly. Instead of covering the imprint of my body in the haphazard fall of snow, I traced the letter B in it and backed away. Let them find it when they felt me transport away, because they *would* find it. Then Matthias would know I was still watching and maybe they'd stay out of my forest.

In the meantime, I had a letter to a Council Member to write.

* * *

Council Member Greyson,

Despite a difficult meeting with the Council, I would like to meet with you in person to discuss the topic of the Sisterhood in greater detail.
Would you be interested?

Sincerely,

Bianca Monroe

* * *

While I waited for Greyson to respond to my missive, I did the only productive thing I could do—attempted to find the demigod with a blue barrette.

Merrick didn't answer his door and hadn't been seen in the castle, so I ventured to other places. My search led me to the upper bailey, where at least two hundred witches milled in a crowd.

I stood on the edge of the Wall, a hood pulled over my face, and silently thanked winter. The cold air and chilly winds gave me plausible disguises that I didn't have to explain away or use magic to create. Instead, I could saunter along the wall in an altered version of Guardian half-armor under my cloak and watch what happened during the winter market.

Or *who* appeared.

The demigods were slippery to track because of their lack of outward differences from witches. Mortals betrayed themselves with their distinctly golden eye color and occasionally variegated hair. Demigods betrayed themselves only by their amulets. Which meant that I didn't hunt demigods.

I hunted amulets.

If god magic activated in my body when I was around other amulets—like when I saw Baxter or the demigod with the blue barrette—then that meant I detected other god magic.

I should be able to *feel* another amulet near me. How close, I didn't know, but I wanted to test the theory now more than ever. The demigod female in Chatham City supported this assumption.

God magic was fickle and unpredictable. Or perhaps it was the goddess magic responding *to* the god magic. I lived in the shades of gray between the two.

The hope of detecting god magic led me to walk through Alkarra often. I strolled through markets in the Southern Network several times a week, or the Northern Network celebrations to welcome winter. The populated areas of the West, or the far reaches of the East.

Today, I waited at the castle to see who showed up. Rarely did a glimpse of heat find me here; amulets hadn't come close to the castle, unless you counted Baxter's, but the demigod with the blue barrette had me curious.

No flickers of god magic stirred in my blood so far, but I

wanted to keep my high vantage point. It allowed me to see more witches. I raked my eyes through those present, searching for glimpses of color in an otherwise dingy day. Snow trickled down from the sky in intermittent, unclear bursts.

No movement here.

Years ago, Papa had convinced Mildred to open the upper bailey to a winter market like this. *Witches gossip like old hens,* he'd told me once, half-laughing. *Why not let them gossip where we can hear them?*

The presence of a witch strolling near the edge of the market—likely Tysen, the Protector-hopeful—confirmed my suspicions. He would pretend interest in something, listen to the conversation as it happened, then leave. Out of sight, he'd change his appearance, come back, and do the same. It was one way they gleaned local news to keep on top of gossip.

According to rumors I heard through previous Guardian's I'd trained in sword work, a gathering in the West would take place soon. It celebrated a local holiday for a grimoire holding spells that could turn sand into water. In the desert, a lifesaver.

As I pondered how I'd find and quietly attend such an event, a voice pulled me from my thoughts.

"You think very hard today."

Ava stood next to me, a bright smile on her young face. Her hair had been pulled back in its usual conglomeration of braids, opening her strong brow and eyes that were more closely-set than most witches. Her liquid gold eyes peered at me with both curiosity and excitement.

I grinned. "Merry meet, Ava."

"Merry meet, Miss Bianca."

"No, please. Drop the Miss."

"Drop the Miss?" Her brow wrinkled. She looked at her hands, which held onto several small books. Her gaze turned to astonishment. "Drop your name? How?"

The confounding of two languages had been an interesting thing to watch Ava tackle. The idioms of our everyday lives often stumped her, even though her fast mind quickly grasped our words and concepts.

"I meant that you can just call me Bianca."

Understanding illuminated her face. "Oh! Very good. I understand. Thank you. Baxter says I call you *Miss* Bianca."

"When it's the two of us, you can say Bianca. Baxter doesn't need to know."

She grinned wider. "A secret. Very good. Thank you."

I'd spent enough time with her and Baxter to know that these books weren't Alkarran. The thin covers constructed out of some sort of fibrous grass that grew in the land of the gods, Alaysia, wrapped these. They were small, about the size of my hand, and the paper inside thin, like old parchment. The ink they used was brittle and flaked off if touched when it was old and too dry. She handled them carefully, like precious gems.

I nodded to the books. "What have you got there?"

"Books on amulets."

No glimmer of god magic lingered in my body, so I felt no guilt turning away from my perusal of the market.

"Oh?" I faced her, deeply interested now. "Tell me more."

She pointed to me with her free hand. "I found in Alaysia. For you. Traded clothes from Alkarra. Very hard." She sounded stern, almost. Twice now, Baxter used god magic to take Ava back to Alaysia. She never wanted to go for long, and each time she returned, she remained quiet and troubled for several days. Eventually, she brightened back to her usually bubbly self. Rarely did she give any details about her visit.

Now, Ava rolled her lips together, entirely too serious for a girl of eleven.

"These books," she said with great concentration, "have the names and . . places of the amulets. They . . . list them?

Show where they are." Her voice roughened with frustration. "Tell how to find amulets. What demigod holds it."

"Like a catalog?"

"Yes?"

I held out a hand. "May I see one?"

She nodded distractedly and gave me the top one. It was only as thick as my little finger and tattered near the spine, which had been sewn together by something like string, only it seemed more leatherish. I ran my finger over it, curious.

"Seaweed," she said. "From mermaids. They like our grass. They cannot get ah . . . below?"

Stated so matter-of-factly, I absorbed her talk of mermaids with a promise to visit that later. Mermaids.

That was a new one.

"Interesting," I murmured, then flipped the book open so it lay flat against my palm. With the tips of my fingers on the edge of the paper so I didn't touch any ink, I turned through the first couple of pages.

On each page lay a diagram-like structure built of lines. Within the lines were words, written in Alaysian. Charts, basically, but without the bigger framework.

"What does it say?" I asked.

"This is amulet we broke," Ava said. "Mortals they . . . they love the amulets. Much want the god magic. They watch the amulets." She used two fingers near her eyes to emphasize. "Write down who. For how long."

"Are the amulets passed around between demigods?" I asked, perusing another page.

Ava shrugged. "Sometimes. *Monilay mal.* Demigods bad. They are not nice, but sometimes they are nice. To demigods."

"Ah. Demigods aren't nice to mortals, but they're nice to each other?"

She grunted, her lips flattening with a surge of what appeared to be annoyance. A nod accompanied her response.

"Yes."

"Interesting."

I didn't understand the words in the chart, nor what time frame this spanned, but it appeared to be a chronological list of where the amulet had been. Numbers appeared—those were familiar—but I didn't understand their dating system. We classified dates according to seasons and months. Every season had three months. The first month of spring. The second month of spring, the third month of spring. Then summer.

These were . . . named differently, I imagined.

"The amulet we broke?" Ava said. "Luppentonisa." Her lips struggled to form around such a big word.

"Luppentonisa?"

"It means, ah . . . very strong?"

"Powerful?"

"Yes!" she cried. "*Powerful.*" She gestured toward the book without touching it, her hands going up and down. "The first . . . lines?"

"Column." I gestured up and down the page. "This is a column." Then horizontally. "This is a row."

"Cahl-um."

"Correct."

She nodded once. "Column. The place the amulet was ah . . . seen. The next call-umm is the mortal."

"The name of the mortal that saw the amulet?"

Another quick nod. "Yes, yes."

"I see."

Ava pointed out several different names—the same mortal would see the amulet around the same area. The mortal that gathered this information noted all rumors in a separate book, and when they confirmed an amulet location, would then put it in this one.

"Why do mortals care?"

"Babies die." Her nose wrinkled. "Sickness comes. Magic saves us with *sangessa* to the demigods."

"Allegiance?" I guessed.

"Yes, yes. Awl-ee-gens."

"Yes."

"We give awl-ee-gens to the *monilay mal*. They save."

Several facets of life in Alaysia clicked together. Desperation, for one. Mortals tracking magical amulets in case they needed to save themselves or their children. A life of service to a demigod, but access to healing powers. Food. I knew enough about Alaysia to know that only the demigods lived well.

Ava gestured toward the book again. "It is old, yes? He gave it because the amulet gone. Dead. The book has no . . . ah . . ."

"Purpose."

She nodded sharply again. "Yes. No purpose. You have it."

The pages closed as I clasped my hand together. "Thank you, Ava. This is a lovely gift and I will treasure it. Can you get more information about other amulets?"

She shrugged.

"Like maybe which amulets are here?"

She frowned. "I don't know. I can ask Baxter. I could . . . go to Alaysia."

The drop of her voice indicated that was the last thing she wanted to do, so I put a reassuring hand on her shoulder.

"That may not be necessary. It was just an idea. If we know what amulets are here, maybe we can find the demigods sooner."

Ava blinked as she processed through that, and I reminded myself to talk slower for her sake. Eventually, she nodded, but I couldn't tell if she truly comprehended it or not. My hand slid off her shoulder. She'd turned her gaze down to the market, then wrapped a hand over her mouth and giggled.

"Goats." She laughed. "So funny."

Two kids hopped around a pen scattered with straw. Their mother ignored them as they scampered over each other, bleating loudly in offense when one toppled the next. Below us, an angry sheep kicked a cart and upturned it, sending hay flying into the air. I smiled and tucked the book into the pocket of my dress.

"There you are, Ava," drawled a voice to my left. Leda stood next to me, clad in a cloak lined with fur. "I've been looking for you."

Ah, Leda.

The exact witch I had been avoiding since the disastrous Council meeting.

"Miss Leda." Ava curtsied. "Merry meet. I hope you are well."

Pleasure stole across Leda's face at Ava's intentional and measured words. "Well done, Ava! Your manners have come a long way and I'm happy to see you use your greetings so well. It's time for your language lesson. Please, meet me at Scarlett's office. I'll be there in fifteen minutes."

Ava darted off in a flash. She disappeared into the castle, where she used hidden paths to get to where she needed to go. Many staff members had gotten used to her—most ignored her, which didn't bother Ava—but plenty of witches still felt uneasy with a mortal girl around.

Leda turned to me. "It was ideal that Ava would be here with you when I came, but I didn't come for her. I've been sent to let you know that Scarlett would like to see you. But," she continued quietly, "she wishes to come to you outside normal hours. In fact, she's requested to come to your cottage."

"Doesn't want me to be seen near her office?"

Leda pressed her thin lips together and nodded. Beneath the layer of professionalism and pretended disinterest, I thought I saw a spark of disapproval in her gaze. I studied her for a second, then turned my attention back to the gentle scene below.

While I understood Scarlett's reason, perhaps even agreed with it on some level, the sense of rejection still stung.

"Tell her I'll be available this evening," I said.

"I'll relay your message."

She turned to go, but stopped. Her differently-colored eyes found mine, highlighted by the white fur of the hood that lined her cape.

"I heard about the Council meeting," she said. Before I could respond, she held up a hand. "From Hiddleston after a meeting with Greyson's Assistant. He was able to see it through her paths, though I don't know all the details of what was said. What he saw indicated it didn't go well. No one else has mentioned it," she quickly added. "The Council hasn't said anything about your appearance, if you're worried about that. Sounds like a disaster."

My jaw tightened. "An unmitigated disaster. They basically laughed me out of there."

"I'm sorry."

"Thanks."

"And for the record, I understand *why* Scarlett would distance herself from you but . . . I don't necessarily agree with it. What the Council did is bullying, that's all. Eventually, she'll lose political power if she let's them control her that way."

My lips twitched. "Thanks, Leda."

"Our weekly dinner tomorrow evening?"

"Sounds great."

"Michelle requested to host it. I'll let her know you'll be there. Merry part, Bianca."

With that, Leda transported away. I stared at the spot where she'd been, filled with snow and flurries now, and straightened up. Weight came off my shoulders when I realized that Leda had actually given me a gift by not requiring me to recount the Council meeting. She was one less witch I had to explain it to.

A flash of bright blue below caught my eye, but disappeared. I frantically searched through the witches in close proximity, but saw nothing to lead me to believe the amulet—or attached demigod—lay somewhere down there.

Wouldn't I feel it, anyway?

Frustrated, I turned away. Who knew? My assumption that I felt amulets was all speculation. I had no proof, only ideas.

The dull drapery of regular witches in winter—muddy capes and heavy leather boots—gave no exposure to an amulet. No flicker of heat registered in my blood either. A hopeful spotting, but not a real one.

With a heavy sigh, I turned away from the Wall.

Time to transport to the West.

Chapter Six

That night, Scarlett arrived with the gentle rap of knuckles on my door.

I heard the *tap-tap-tap* while rinsing a rag. Grains of sand littered the top of my table as I attempted to clean the Western Network off my boots. Unfortunately, I hadn't taken my sandals to wear when I shuffled around the West, attempting to find a demigod. Like looking for a particular grain of sand in the ocean, really.

"Coming!" I called, and set the boots aside to dry near the fire.

Barefoot, I crossed the cold wooden floor and made a mental note to close Goat into the little barn I'd made her. The night would be chilly.

When I opened the door to admit Scarlett inside, she peered out of a wide hood in a deep red cloak. Snow fell around her shoulders, dripping from branches far, far overhead.

"Bianca."

I opened the door wider. "High Priestess."

"Scarlett, please," she said gently. "We are not at the castle."

With a smile, I amended my greeting. "Scarlett. Please, come in."

Priscilla looked up from where she sat at the fire, hands in her lap and a tired expression on her face. She smiled at Scarlett, who returned it with little surprise.

Scarlett stepped into the room and pushed her cloak off her face. To my shock, her hair was out of its usual bun and loose on her shoulders. Had the world stopped spinning? I'd never heard of Scarlett changing her appearance. Not once.

Thick, dark locks twirled in a haphazard mess, as if she'd unwrapped her braid and ran her fingers through the strands. It dropped almost to her elbow, glossy in the firelight. With it down, she appeared years younger.

How old was she, anyway?

"Scarlett," Priscilla murmured, eyes wide, "your hair is lovely. I don't think I've ever seen it down before."

Silently, I echoed Priscilla's thoughts. Once, maybe, in a braid, when caught in a moment of surprise before she was ready for work, but even that could have been my imagination.

A wry smirk crossed Scarlett's expression. "Thank you. I wouldn't usually be so informal but . . . I view you more as daughters than professional politicians. I have a walloping headache," she admitted, and the strain in her eyes was more than obvious. "I pulled my hair down on my way here and already feel some relief. Let's just say that things have been . . . extra consuming these days."

The door closed behind her with a firm *thunk*, as if to punctuate her thoughts.

"Let your hair down with us anytime," I said with a wry smile that she returned, even if half-heartedly. "Please have a seat by the fire. It's cold out there."

A spell sent more wood onto the dying flames, and within

Obviously, she'd also changed her appearance, perhaps to observe first.

Had she forgotten that I could see her, just like in the South?

I fiddled with the edge of my *Chatham Chatterer* scroll as I pretended to peruse it. Instead, I attempted another message to Leda. The moment I issued the spell, all the candles extinguished along our wall.

Several eyes drifted our way, but I simply looked at the candles, acting equally astonished. Moments later they bounced back to life and the hubbub continued at the same low tone as before. Except the tension in the room ratcheted up. Patrons along the wall stood with tense shoulders. Gazes darted around.

A shot of dread filled my stomach with a new thought.

"How many witches do you see here?" I asked quietly.

The response came on my parchment.

Eight.

My heart skipped a beat when I counted at least twenty. The good gods.

Did that mean at least twelve demigods were here?

I swallowed back my rising fear. Not only could I not see Tipa here, but now I'd called other demigods to the Golden Guinea Hen. Oh, my plan had worked all right.

A little *too* well.

"Jikes," I whispered.

What would I do against twelve demigods? Leda wrote another message.

How many do you see?

"Twenty," I murmured.

Total silence answered behind me. Not even the scratch of a quill or gentle rub of tweed on wood as she readjusted. Leda had gone utterly still.

Ten minutes now before Papa and Baxter were "scheduled" to arrive and see my new, broken amulet. They wouldn't. But on or before that minute, I'd have to make a decision.

Approach the demigod on the other side of the room or get out of here?

My heart pounded as I thought it over.

Every now and then, I glanced outside. Snow had begun to fall. The street was clear, as if witches scuttled inside to get away from whatever lay in the air. The Chatterer had nothing else to report, either. More demigod speculation, but the articles recycled the same old rumors over and over again.

A tiny tear in the scroll elongated as I rubbed my finger along the edge. The flickering, steady heat in my blood grew again until I felt warm enough to be uncomfortable. The magic wouldn't burn me, so to speak, but the building power couldn't be ignored.

So many demigods.

I glanced around, but no one had entered through the front door. Movement drew my gaze to the left.

A woman descended spiraling stairs near the back corner. She stepped through a doorway now, a silk purple gown rustling around her legs. It slipped over the floor like loose liquid, easily moving.

Elegance aside, there was a sense of something else *odd* about the dress.

The cut, perhaps. The style? Maybe her general air and demeanor. Whatever I sensed in her, it didn't feel native to the Central Network. To Alkarra, even.

Her gaze briefly landed on mine. When I caught it, the skin between her brows puckered. Thin lips disappeared into a line as she settled at the bar next to the man, yanking my thoughts out of their confusing path. I tore a piece of the *Chatterer* off, yanked a pencil from my bag, and scrawled, *Cast a spell on me that will increase my hearing.*

Then I balled it up and tossed it over my shoulder.

Let it land, I chanted in my head. *Let her see it.*

Moments later, the general sounds of the inn were magnified. My heart raced. It had worked! The good gods bless Leda and her detail-orientedness.

While I locked my gaze outside, my attention spun back to the demigods, now able to hone in on the throaty voice of the male demigod next to the woman that had just descended.

"Are you ready?" he asked.

"It's not about us," she replied coolly. "We need this to move fast or we're going to be late and that would not be a welcomed thing. Not tonight."

"It's worth it."

"Better be."

He made a sound in his throat, not unlike the ones Ava did on occasion. Another fake sip of ipsum. As he set the cup down, he murmured, "Think it's true?"

"I hope not."

"Unnerving," he muttered. "Isn't she?"

"She saw me."

"She sees all of us."

"How?"

He shrugged. "Soon, it won't matter."

The female demigod put her back to me, an elegant line of beads racing from her waist to the top of her shoulder. The same draw existed in her, equally potent with the two of them together, but I ignored it for the more obvious point.

The worst-case scenario had just happened. I hadn't drawn Tipa to the Golden Guinea Hen.

I'd drawn others instead.

Were they children of Gelas? Ignis? Tontes? Why did they care about the amulet I claimed to have broken?

Why were so many of them here?

A body moved in front of a window on the opposite side of the room. I glanced over, startled to see Tipa walking by. She peered inside, then straight ahead. Moments later, she appeared near another window.

Her gaze met mine. She frowned and disappeared.

All my control kept me from calling out to her, asking her to come back.

Jikes.

The plan began to crumble before my very eyes. Tipa left, other demigods remained in unprecedented numbers. I sat here with an old-man version of Leda and no plan for what to do next.

If I left, would I waste a golden opportunity to prove the Sisterhood?

Absolutely.

If I left, would I possibly spare my own life?

Also absolutely.

A crash from the back room ripped through my ears. I tightened my lips to prevent a grimace. "Stop the spell," I hissed, pretending to scratch my ear.

Seconds later, it faded.

While I recovered from seeing Tipa, I pretended to study the scroll. Another message appeared from Leda.

Three minutes. Are there more?

"Yes," I murmured.

Why don't I see them? There's hardly anyone here.
Several just left and I see only two other witches.

I sucked in a sharp breath. That meant nearly *all* patrons were demigods. My palms began to sweat. The good gods. Twenty demigods.

A plan. I needed a new plan.

Really, one opportunity to touch an amulet would get me what I needed. Another amulet would answer so many questions. It would create more fear of witches, less amulets available.

An accidental trip is all it took. Someone shoving me into a demigod where I could then grab a hidden amulet . . . it could be so simple.

One minute. Is Tipa here?

"Not anymore," I whispered low.

My stomach turned itself over, threatening to flip. Another quick review of the room, as if I were impatient for Papa to arrive, sent my heart to racing. So many eyes peered at me now. Most didn't even try to hide it.

Eyes from *everywhere*.

Across the room. Near the door. At the bar—on both sides. Sitting at a table in the middle. The serving girl that brought me water. They didn't stare in an unbroken way, but looked at me frequently enough to leave no doubt.

Fear should have taken my breath away. Should have shocked me into the stupidity of this plan, helped me see that I could get away now before any lines were crossed. Any graves dug.

But I didn't let it.

A new plan had cobbled together, hastily and imperfect, but something.

"Time," the old man murmured.

"I'm doing it," I whispered.

Instead of cowering, I slipped out of the booth and gained my feet.

"Don't do this," the old man whispered, his voice brittle as burnt paper. "This was a mistake. I can't help you if I can't see them."

Too late, I thought.

"It'll be fine," I whispered. "I have a plan. Get into place now, like we planned for an emergency escape. I have a feeling we'll need it."

The old man disappeared.

When I drew my shoulders back, attaining my full height, the bearded male at the bar stood. I met his gaze. My chin notched up. The presence of so many amulets brought fire to life in my blood, like a boiling whirlpool.

Matthias's voice tumbled around my mind as I faced the hostile demigod, and the equally curious female demigod next to him.

While important, Matthias had said, *you were not instrumental.*

Well, we'd see about that now.

The entire pub studied me now, as if sizing me up. I could practically hear their thoughts. This *is the amulet-breaker?* they seemed to say.

"You know what we want," the male said. He spoke like a gravel slide down a mountain. Rough. Clattering. Destructive.

Standing gave me a better look at him. Strong through the legs, thick in the arms and shoulders. His heightened strength would only be assisted by muscles so sculpted.

My right hand went to my pocket, fingers curling around the amulet inside. They openly watched me now, and I cataloged at least twenty. Each of them followed the movement of my hand to the amulet.

With their distraction, I studied as many of them as I could. No one wore any obvious amulets. I'd have to find out which of them—perhaps all of them—had an amulet, then go for the easiest.

Close proximity, I told myself in a reassuring chant. *All I need is close proximity and a good fight. That's it.*

My nails ached because I held onto the fake amulet so hard. The rug shifted slightly beneath my boots, preparing with my thoughts.

"You want it?" I murmured with a smile. "Come and get it."

A window banged open behind me as the Volare rose from beneath my feet and swept me into the air.

* * *

Wintry air rushed over me as the Volare cocooned me, then flew outside. The sheer unexpectedness bought me a few moments of time to get into Letum Wood and take the fight there, where the trees could help.

One second I stared at the golden glow of the upper floor, the next second something tackled me.

I shouted as a demigod landed on my back. We slammed into the ground, pinned by their weight—or maybe magic.

The Volare struggled to free itself, but it was no match for the demigod.

"Not so fast," a male growled in my ear. The one from the bar. He gripped my body in iron-like arms; my ribs were at the breaking point. He stood up with me wrapped in a vise-like grip.

"Go!" I yelled to the Volare. "Stay with Leda."

I'd rather revise my plan again than lose my magical rug to a demigod.

The Volare zipped away, taking to the air. Thanks to god magic, I stood back in the Golden Guinea Hen a second later.

Legs flailing, I lashed out. The shaggy serving girl that told me about the soup was my closest target. A second before my foot would have connected with her nose, she disappeared, then reappeared a few paces back.

Ah.

She had an amulet.

The demigod tightened his hold around my chest, pinning my arms to my side. My right hand remained in my pocket, my left near my waist. Thready breaths were all I could manage. If he wanted, he could crack my spine in half.

He wrestled me closer to the booth where I'd been sitting.

"Calm down, witch," he hissed. "Give us what we want and we'll leave you alone."

I went limp and hung my head, as if giving up. He grunted. The moment his guard lowered, I slammed my head back as hard as I could. Something crunched beneath my skull and I hoped it was his nose.

He squealed, releasing me.

The impact of his head against mine sent a tremor through my brain, but I blinked it off. The demigod collapsed to the ground.

I ripped my right hand out of the cape, grabbed my knife with my left hand, spun around, and faced the rest of them in a ready crouch. The replica of Nicomedianthekus lay in my open palm and drew every eye in the room.

"Are you ready for the same thing to happen to your amulet?" I called.

Nearly twenty demigods stared at me in varying stages of shock, rage, and uncertainty. Three of them immediately disappeared. Another hesitated, on the brink.

The stocky male writhed on the ground, hand on his face, muttering in a different language. Blood poured out between his fingers.

The fake amulet pulsed in my hand, except for a streak of black that crossed it in a slash similar to what happened to

Luppontonisa. For added effect, I'd put a spell on it to mimic a burn, but without heat. Now, a little trace of smoke trailed out of it, as if the wound were still fresh. My already-issued, established magic, apparently, still worked around so many amulets.

The woman that stood at the bar gasped. Another one let out a cry. Somewhere at the back of the crowd, a glass crashed to the ground.

I held the amulet higher.

"One step closer," I hissed, then motioned to the demigod posing as the serving girl, "and I'll destroy her amulet the same way. I know she has one with her."

She recoiled, then stiffened, arms at her side. Her wary gaze regarded me with a deep hatred. Several of them shuffled back a step. My back hit the edge of the booth as I snarled. Blood dripped on the shirt of the demigod I'd hit with my head. It had a shimmery quality, different from ours.

"We're going to do this my way," I murmured. "First, you're going to make me a magical promise to never come back to Alkarra. Then, I'm going to let you leave with all your amulets intact. Those of you that have one with you, anyway," I added, sending a glare to a demigod in front.

Her too-attractive cheekbones, full lips, and wild, spiraling black tresses in a halo around her hair were a dead-giveaway that she wasn't using magic to appear different.

She bared her teeth.

Another voice came from the back. "That's not how this will work."

A woman stepped forward, sauntering with the hush of shoes on the wooden floor. Instead of a dress, she wore black pants with so much material it looked like a dress. Silver and gold thread wound through the shoulders, extending all the way to her wrists.

Her hair, a gentle auburn, piled on top of her head. Around her neck lay a bright pink amulet so electric it was difficult to gaze on. Fluid colors of red and a pale peach appeared around the edges of the triangular face.

She stopped only a few paces away, just out of reach.

"Daughter of Ignis?" I guessed. "I assumed the god of thunder would be a bit darker with his other amulets. Maybe black. Like the souls of his children."

She lifted a perfectly-arched eyebrow. "My father is not your concern," she murmured and sent a lazy glance out the door. "We can talk about amulet colors, or we can talk about Alkarra. Are you aware of what's happening out there?"

A growing silence allowed me to refocus my attention. Outside, screams sounded. Distant flashes of light. I didn't dare look to the side just in case this was an attempt to distract me. The urge to see it was nearly overwhelming.

I ignored it to study this new demigod. She had a disconcerting confidence that gave me a moment of doubt. If she called my bluff and touched the amulet, what would I do against seventeen demigods?

I sent a hasty glance to the male with the broken, bloody nose. He stood, blood staining his chin and teeth as he scowled at me. The nose appeared to be repairing itself, even if the bloodstains remained behind.

Some of them were angry enough to kill me already.

The sheer number of amulets ratcheted my blood to a frenzy. The fever pitch sent cascades of flame through me. If I wanted, I felt I could take flight.

"Alkarra is about to fall to our command," she murmured. "As we speak, the demigod uprising is falling into place. Our leader is about to breach Chatham Castle. You are one little girl, but we are many. Is this really a fight you want to waste your time with right now? Or should you be out saving Alkarra?"

Like sand beneath my feet, everything began to slip away. My plan. My hope for the Sisterhood.

My Network.

"Demigod uprising?" I whispered.

A cold smile crossed her lips, like a shadow.

"Alkarra will be ours by the time the night is through."

"Why do you want Alkarra?"

She almost laughed, but caught it. It would have been a cold scoff.

"Because," she murmured, "you have everything here."

"Everything," I hissed, leaning closer, "including goddesses and amulet-breakers. We're not going down without a fight. Some of us are goddess-touched, you know?"

Her expression faltered with uncertainty, then deadpanned. Hiddleston and Leda had debated over whether being goddess-touched *actually* meant anything at all, but at the moment, I didn't care. I had to bluff my way through this, and invoking a goddess seemed the most likely next step, regardless of truth.

The careful, precise tone of her voice dropped to a whisper that every single demigod present must have heard.

"We," she murmured, "aren't frightened of you."

"You should be," I whispered.

She advanced toward me with a scowl.

I flung the amulet as hard as I could. It slammed into her chest, throwing her back against the rest of them. She gasped, sucking in a deep breath, as her sternum crackled beneath the hit. I crouched to fight, my body tense. Useless curses lingered on the tip of my tongue as I faced a room of shocked demigods.

Just as the brawny male lunged for me a second time, magic from somewhere whisked me away.

Chapter Seventeen

woman hidden behind a heavy sapphire hood stood at my side.

Chatham City unfolded around us, near the middle of the city, where buildings nearly stacked on top of each other. Smoke choked the air, thick and noxious. My head spun, dizzy from the unexpected, though welcome, change of scenery.

The hidden witch held onto my arm, clutching me firmly. Tipa's melodic voice inquired, "Are you absolutely insane?"

Screams echoed down the thin street. My mind bobbled around, disoriented. Chaos unfurled. Desperation and fear permeated the air. I glanced around to realize we weren't far from the castle.

A witch sprinted by, calling at the top of his lungs, "The demigods are here! The demigods are here! Get into your homes and hide!"

Witches ran from house to house, knocking on doors. Some screamed from the windows to witches in the streets. Others cried. A young child scrambled into a barrel and yanked the top over himself.

Down the way, witches—demigods?—with torches strode down the road, as if they owned the place. Four or five of them sent balls of fire into nearby houses, torching them instantly. Flames grew high and hot.

The blood drained from my face. "The good gods," I whispered.

They hadn't been kidding.

The demigod uprising had arrived.

The hood moved back slightly, revealing Tipa's grim expression.

"Let's go," she muttered. "We need to talk."

I swallowed hard. "Go where? We have to stop this."

"Because you stopped them so easily at the Golden Guinea Hen?" she snapped. "The children of Ignis have decided to take over Alkarra. I saved you from a very idiotic thing and now we are going to *try* to save Alkarra. Do you understand? There is no guarantee. Without me, you have *no* hope."

"Right," I snapped back. "I'm just supposed to trust you, another demigod?"

"Do you have a choice?" she hissed. "Didn't I just save you from a very unsavory death?"

I hesitated. *Could* I trust her?

Could I not?

Her gaze was earnest. Firm. Annoyed even. Some quiet quality in there reminded me of Baxter.

"No," I muttered. "I suppose I don't have a choice."

She arched her brow. "Do you promise not to break my amulet?"

I nodded.

"Then let's go. We have things to do."

* * *

No visible tension gave Tipa away as anything but calm, except for a slight tightening around the back of her shoulders. Hints of dark hair appeared beneath her cloak, peeking out in gentle waves at her shoulders.

The god magic inside me roiled with her close presence, teeming in a bright whirl. Up until now, I hadn't been this close to or touched by any demigod that wasn't Baxter. Tipa's presence felt more intense.

Agitated, perhaps.

Within the whirling burn of god magic came other spurts of fire. Heat. Trembling. Like god magic activated in spurts, or different demigods appeared here and there that I couldn't see.

"We need to get you somewhere safe," she murmured, "and we have very little time to do it. The only reason I brought you to this part of your city is because I wanted you to see what's happening. You wouldn't have believed me otherwise."

"True."

"It's worse everywhere else. They saved Chatham City and the castle for the final push."

"Your demigod brothers and sisters?" I snapped.

Her lips thinned. "No," she muttered. "Not mine. We have nothing to do with Ignis and his wild children."

As she spoke, she strode quickly. We cut through the gathering crowds of fleeing witches headed for Letum Wood. She steered us to the right until Chatham Castle became visible ahead, a dark specter of stone set against an almost-darker sky.

I sucked in a sharp breath.

The portcullis was down. Guardians lined the Wall. Archers stood on top of turrets, bows at the ready. Torches burned bright and hot above and below the Wall, illuminating the ground in better light. A familiar horn rippled through the air, deep, resonant, and terrifying. My blood turned to slush at the sound. The last time I'd heard it had been during the War of the Networks, right before the final battle. The sound clattered my teeth all the way to my jaw.

"Are they going to attack the castle?" I whispered.

"If they must." She glanced my way, revealing a hint of a strong jaw as she added with a wry aside. "If Bram can guarantee his success another way, he will. He wants to keep the castle as intact as possible. Apparently, he wants it to be his own."

Fury bubbled up in me. "Bram!" I hissed. "Bram is leading this?"

"He's an unfortunate thorn in everyone's side."

"I knew it!" I cried. "I knew he wouldn't get punished, and now he's back. We should have killed him when we had the chance."

"With any luck," she muttered, then nudged me to the left, "you'll get another chance."

We crossed a street and headed into the forest. The frightened Tipa that had fled from my side several times had disappeared. She appeared cool and collected tonight. Perhaps, like me, she did better under pressure.

Unable to help myself, I said, "You're not afraid of me anymore."

Her jaw ticked slightly. "Afraid isn't the right word."

"You disappeared twice around me. I wanted to talk to you at the castle in the South, you know."

"I protected my amulet."

"So why did you believe me when I said I wouldn't hurt your amulet today?"

"Because you're just about to lose everything," she murmured. "Before tonight, I didn't have the luxury of collateral."

I swallowed past my pride and said, "Thank you for saving me, by the way. I . . . I needed help back there and I appreciate you giving it. I got in over my head."

Tipa said nothing, but turned to the side to dodge a swiftly moving cart, packed with children. A horse trotted toward the forest, eyes wild. The owner's arms strained as they tried to control the animal, clucking harried reassurances as babies wailed in the back.

A nearby roof illuminated the night sky with flames. The silhouette of a witch transporting on top, dousing it with a spell, and then leaving followed. My throat thickened.

A Protector, for certain.

We walked alone toward the castle. A line of ten Guardians formed a wall near the upper bailey entrance. Likely, there were more that we couldn't see. From what I could tell, no attack had started on the castle yet.

A hopeful sign.

"Your house is here, right?" she asked, one hand gesturing toward the forest. "In the forest close to the castle?"

"It's in Letum Wood, but not right here."

She growled. "I thought it was right next to the castle!"

I laughed, but it had little humor. "You couldn't pay me to live next to the castle. I live farther into the forest."

"We need to go there."

"Why?"

Her jaw clenched and nostrils flared. "To keep you *safe*, like I said. Think of your cottage in your mind. I can touch you and read your thoughts."

My eyes widened. "What?"

"Just do it!"

I hesitated. "That's my home. My only safe spot. I'm not telling you where it is. We're safe enough in Letum Wood. The trees will protect me."

"*You* are not safe anywhere but you have the best shot at your house. You said you'd trust me."

"Then tell me why you're helping us," I countered.

Tipa hesitated. "Let's just say that my father has a vested interest in Alkarra not falling to pieces."

"Why?"

She growled. "I'm not saying anymore. Let's go."

"Then no deal."

She stopped to stare at me, shocked. "No deal?" she murmured. "You're saying no to me when I'm offering to save your *world*."

"At your own gain, I presume."

Tipa's rage smoldered like a hot coal. A loud cry issued from the city, then another. Breaking glass sounded from not far away. A flash of movement from the Wall caught my eye. Archers turned toward Chatham road, where a line of demigods appeared with more fire. Her gaze darted back, then over to me again.

I leaned forward and whispered, "Never trust a demigod," with Ava in mind.

Tipa's expression cycled through frustration, annoyance, and finally resignation before she let out a sharp hiss.

"Fine! You want to know? Here it is. You have become the first living amulet in all of history. That's right. *You* are a witch and a god magic amulet. The moment the sons and daughters of Ignis understand what you are, they will stop at nothing to have you. How they haven't figured it out yet, I have *no* idea."

Shock held my throat captive for a full ten seconds.

Living amulet?

Before I could recover my thoughts enough to respond, she pushed me off to the side, near a cluster of bushes. An empty footpath headed toward Letum Wood, and she hurried onto it. The bushes bent closer, scraping my legs.

"An amulet," I murmured.

"Fortunately for you," Tipa sent me a sharp glare, "I don't think his demigods have figured it out yet. Not entirely, anyway, though they're on the right track. You calling them into the Golden Guinea Hen with a false amulet certainly didn't help."

"It was meant for you!"

"Well, you didn't control the variables well enough! Now they're curious. Me saving you may have them already thinking that *you* did god magic." She growled low in her throat. "I don't know what they know! But whatever it is, it isn't good."

In the background, the trees hummed, louder than ever. Branches rustled as we sped past, clattering in the night. The Guardians watching from the Wall didn't seem to notice as we disappeared into the shadows, though the trees as they moved out of my way were a dead giveaway.

"You must be kidding," I finally rasped. "A living amulet? God magic? That . . . it doesn't make sense."

"Get used to it," she muttered.

I opened my mouth to protest again, but stopped. *The first living amulet.* Of course. The puzzle slid together as I thought it out. God magic lived inside me, as if I contained it. I detected other amulets, because god magic must recognize itself. In some strange, desperate way, it *did* make sense.

"Amulet," I whispered.

She sighed, a rough sound that was more long-suffering than regret.

"Amulet," she confirmed. "Something none of us expected, if I'm to be honest. And I've seen many wild things. I don't think the gods even know what to make of you."

Despite the blow of terrifying news, I felt marginally safer back in the forest. Now, Letum Wood could watch what happened around me that I couldn't see. The voices of the trees rose from the back of my mind, frantic from the chaos in the city now. All I heard was a high-pitched, panicked hum, so I mentally set them aside.

"Let's say it's true." I darted to keep up with her swift

pace. "What does it mean if I *am* an amulet?"

"It means three things. First, the only way to get the god magic removed is to approach Ignis. He'll have to take his magic back for it to leave you."

The sound of his name sent a shudder through me. "Ominous," I muttered. "And second?"

"The children of Ignis will be coming for you as soon as they figure it out, which could be any moment now."

"Double ominous. What's third?"

She paused, shoved a tree branch out of the way, and glanced back over her shoulder. An uneasy expression lingered there.

"You might be able to use god magic."

I gasped.

Tipa studied me, then plunged back into the forest. "You better hope you can. Whatever happens tonight, trust one thing: if the demigods get you back to Alaysia tonight, then there's no hope for Alkarra."

"Why?"

She batted aside a vine that had fallen. It swung against a tree and stuck there, leaving ample room for me to pass by unbothered.

"The demigods will start to turn against each other. They'll fight over you because you're bound to have more power than any gem could hold. They'll hope that you are the key to them accessing goddess magic and will take you back to the gods. The last thing we need is for you to be in front of Ignis right now. He's bound to be too confident. He'll act rashly. Tontes will try to have you for himself and a war will break out. History has seen it before."

I attempted to use a spell to put my wild hair into a braid, but a nearby branch cracked instead. Frustrated, I shoved the strands back out of my eyes and attempted to keep up with her long strides. I trotted behind her.

"If this uprising is also successful and the demigods control witches in Alkarra," she continued, "it could also become the catalyst for the war of the gods. The four gods will fracture into two groups and fight each other. Worse case scenario? The goddess sisters get involved."

She shuddered.

"War of the gods," I muttered. "Jikes. Then tell me how to do god magic. Teach me and I can help you stop Ignis and his children!"

Tipa paused inside the forest and turned around to face me. Her hood slipped off her head, giving way to her full blonde-and-brown locks.

"I don't have time to teach you god magic. It's not that complicated, but it takes some work. It's . . . intent based. Anyway, I'm here to keep you safe on orders given by my father. Once you're home, I will attempt to stop the demigod uprising tonight. Then I'll come back for you and we'll discuss it, all right? We don't have time for this. Picture your house. I can take us to it from here."

My hands felt shaky as I shoved my hair out of my face again. I didn't have a choice. I had to trust Tipa. Being a living amulet put me in over my head. She wasn't a friend, but I couldn't peg her as an enemy either. For now, it would have to be enough.

With great reluctance I said, "Fine."

Her fingers impatiently curled into her palms in a hurried gesture. I lifted my hand, pictured my cottage, and felt the cool touch of her palm on my arm. A pause, then I opened my eyes.

I stood in front of my home, disoriented a second time.

Goddess magic transportation involved the whole body. Pressure. Incantations. Awareness. Intention. The process was preparation for the change in position and scenery. With god magic, the change happened as instantly as a blink.

My god magic sloshed around, churning and hot

Tipa gestured to my door with a tip of her head, her hair a waterfall of color as it brushed her shoulders.

"Get inside," she ordered. "And don't leave. I have to go find Baxter and his sisters and then I'll be back."

"You can't be serious. You want me to stay here while Alkarra burns?"

"You're a living amulet," she hissed through clenched teeth. "I am very serious. I have three other demigods that will help me do this—if Baxter is even available and his ridiculous sisters agree—and *no* time to take care of you. Now go!"

"But I should be out there!" I cried. "I need to be helping, not hiding. If I really can do god magic, then I should."

A press of magic shoved me against my door with a thud. Rage bloomed in her eyes as she stepped up to where she'd pinned me to the door, a finger pointed right in my face.

"The demigods will salivate over you and then create a war between the gods," she ground out, voice low and terrifying. "Do you not *get* that? If the gods go to war, Alaysia will be destroyed. Whatever demigods survive it will invade Alkarra to live. If you think half of Ignis' children are a problem right now, wait until the ruthless children of Tontes get involved too. Some demigods will save their mortals and invade *your* land with them. When the gods are angry, hurricanes surge and waves crash and thunder doesn't stop and fire consumes the land and all of Alkarra will be affected by the wrath of the gods."

My nostrils flared as I studied her. The fear in her eyes convinced me that what she said was true. I shoved aside the bubbling fear.

This was going nowhere. Until I agreed to her terms, we'd only waste time. "Fine," I muttered.

With that, she put me in the middle of my house with god magic and disappeared.

Chapter Eighteen

I t took all of fifteen seconds for me to collect my breath, think through my immediate options, and transport away.

Thankfully, Tipa left no residual magic to hold me in, so I went to the only place I could fathom going next.

Papa's apartment.

My mind spun as I landed in the hallway. I rapped on the door, mildly concerned I'd dreamed the whole thing. Reeves opened it, made a sound in his throat that indicated some relief at seeing me, and stepped aside to allow me in. Whispers of heat and fire slipped through my blood every now and then. Nothing frightening, but a stark difference to the bright illuminations of Letum Wood.

Before I could ask about Papa, Reeves motioned across the room.

A weary figure sat at an oblong table, his head in his hands. Papa had run his fingers through his hair, then stopped, tangling them in the thick strands. He stared at the empty table top, as ragged as I'd ever seen him. I stepped farther into the room.

"Papa?"

He straightened, met my gaze, and quietly asked, "Have you heard?"

I swallowed. "I was out in the city. It's . . . utter madness."

He stood and trapped me in a long hug. When I pulled away, I saw his exhaustion up close.

"I'm surprised you're here," I admitted quietly. "I thought you'd be out there."

He scoffed. "I'm not here because I desire to be stuck in an office while demigods rampage Alkarra, that's for sure. But my plan with Scarlett is in place and I'm committed to seeing it through. Just . . . rallying my courage now, I suppose. I've summoned Scarlett and Marten to my office. Matthias will arrive there soon."

"What of Talmund?" I asked, thinking of the Head of Guardians.

"He's out," he muttered grimly, "Doing what I want to do. Come with me and we'll see what they have to say."

I stopped Papa with a hand on his arm.

"Papa, what is your plan?"

He hesitated, ran his bottom lip through his teeth, then let out a long sigh.

"The demigod problem is beyond me, Bianca. The Council doesn't trust me. They are trying to tie my hands out of fear and a desire to wrest control. Meanwhile, the demigods had open access to our Network. Now they are kidnapping our Coven Leaders and Council Members with thought magic that we're too slow to combat. This is an enemy we've never fought before, and nothing I throw at them is working. They've started their offensive push, and we can't match it."

We didn't even know half of it yet, I had a feeling. Seeing doubt in Papa's expression was enough to send a stab of disbelief and fear through me.

"You've never let us down, Papa. You won't tonight."

He gave a weary smile and tucked me into his side. "I trust that is true, regardless of the path. Come, B. Let's see what Marten and Scarlett and Matthias have to say. It seems like the right thing to have you at my side, tonight of all nights."

With those grim words in the air, I followed him into the hallway.

* * *

Conversation greeted us as we stepped into Papa's office. Scarlett, Marten, Aldred, and Matthias stood in a scattered mix near Papa's fireplace, where warm fire cast light into the dim room. Candles and lamps bounced to life, flooding the space. Matthias sent me a questioning, troubled look that I acted like I didn't see.

"Where is Baxter?" Papa asked.

The tired witch from our apartment had transformed with every step on the walk over. His booming voice had command again, and I saw every bit of the leader we needed Papa to be.

Marten murmured, "I've sent for him."

"Thank you."

"He's probably part of this," Aldred muttered, earning a murderous look from Papa.

I remained back as Papa stood behind his desk, leaned his hands into the top, and peered at those gathered.

A shuffle of shadows moved to the side. Leda stepped up next to me, clad in a dark gray dress and a solemn expression. The Volare appeared from where it hovered behind her. In a snap, it rolled itself into a tight bundle and flopped at my feet. I sent it into the case with a spell, relieved to have it back.

"You're alright?" I asked Leda.

"I've been worried," she whispered. "Where did you—"

"You did great. Thank you for opening the window and letting the Volare follow you."

She hesitated, then nodded. Her face had gone pale, her lips pinched as if she wanted to vomit at any moment. She clutched three large scrolls to her chest, crushing the delicate paper. Before she could speak, Papa's voice broke the air.

"Give me what updates you have, Matthias," he said.

Leda's half-open mouth snapped shut. I reached over and squeezed her hand. She returned the gesture.

"Demigods are on the rise in the Central Network," Matthias said. "Presumably all of Alkarra. Council Member Rosanna has been kidnapped. Martha and Xander are confirmed gone, but we're still getting details. Sounds like the demigods went into their houses and just . . . took them out."

"The majority of demigods are presumed to be in the Southern Network," Marten interjected, "but reports are difficult to obtain."

Matthias nodded, then gestured to some scrolls on Papa's desk.

"Talmund's latest report just arrived. He said that we've sent further Guardians to protect Alina, and requested those Guardians who are present in the South to report immediately. The East is also reporting kidnapped leaders, but not letting us know to what extent. As far as we know, Niko Aldana is safe."

"The West?" Papa asked, looking to Scarlett.

"Four leaders taken already. Lana is safe, protected by West Guards in an unknown location."

"Any High Priests or High Priestesses taken?"

Marten shook his head. "None reported so far."

"Estimated number of demigods?" Papa asked.

He opened a drawer, rooted inside for a moment, and extracted a small key. Aldred's beady eyes tapered down as Papa moved.

Matthias spoke this time, but more haltingly. "Still not sure on numbers. We're assuming at least fifty, but it's a low estimation. Could be twice that. So far, the targets are mostly leaders. We haven't had any reports of witches being taken that aren't in leadership positions."

"Matthias," Papa said, straightening. "Tell Talmund to have his Guardians here leave the Wall and retreat. We're closing down the castle from within."

Matthias blinked. "You want me to tell the Head of Guardians to break our first line of defense?"

"I do. While he's doing that, bring all our Council Members, Coven Leaders, and other ancillary leaders into the castle that we can find. Station four Guardians at each opening. Without the Wall to cover, it will be easier to guard all leaders."

"So many leaders here?" Matthias asked.

"Yes."

"Is it wise to have them in one location?"

"If we spread them out, we cannot protect them all. The demigods will take all they can get their hands on."

He hesitated, then nodded. "Yes, Your Highness."

Papa unlocked another drawer and rummaged around inside, eventually extracting a worn, wooden box. Inscriptions filled the outside. He set it on the table, the key placed on top. Then he braced both hands on either side of the box and turned to Aldred.

"Establish some rooms for the leadership coming in, Aldred. Their families may come as well. Please make sure they're comfortable. Come up with a system to keep everyone up-to-date but no panic, please."

Aldred opened his mouth to protest, then hesitated. "But that's the housekeeper's job," he stammered. "What if they come for me while I'm doing that? I need to . . . I don't know . . ."

Papa glared at him from beneath a menacing brow. "Then find the housekeeper and have it done," he murmured silkily.

"You're the self-appointed head of the Council, are you not? Take care of your Council then, as you desire."

I bit back a whoop.

Aldred nodded. "Yes, Your Highness. I only—"

"Not a word, Aldred." The finality in Papa's voice rang through the room. "Your time to rise as leader has almost passed, and you've shown your true colors to those who matter. See to it, now. Leda, Bianca, Matthias, you are excused. Scarlett, Marten, remain behind."

"What is your father doing?" Leda murmured, eyes narrowed on the box on top of the table. "Is that . . .? No. It couldn't be. He . . ."

She trailed away, shaking her head as if she couldn't believe what she saw. Her knuckles turned white clutching the scrolls, which had buckled underneath her fingers.

Aldred huffed past me, muttering under his breath. I ignored him, my mind caught up in spiraling loops of thought.

Demigods.

Cleverness.

Alkarra.

Leda looked at the box on the desk, hesitated, then followed as I turned out the door. Just before we left, I glanced back.

Papa and Marten spoke so quietly I couldn't hear what they said, but the mournful expression on Marten's face made my stomach catch. As if he felt my gaze, Papa turned. He saw me staring and his expression softened. A semblance of a smile appeared there, then disappeared, as fleeting as grace.

With a nod, he motioned me out the door.

Leda's perplexed expression followed in the hallway. I ignored it, my mind populating with a new idea. Halfway back to Papa's apartment, I slowed. Leda mirrored my pace until we stopped completely.

She lifted her head and asked in a small voice, "What is your father about to do, Bianca?"

"I don't know. I don't have time to consider that right now."

She opened her mouth, then stopped. Her eyes tapered. "What?" she demanded. "What does that expression you have mean?"

"I have an idea."

She tilted her head to the side, then her eyes widened. "Bianca Monroe," she cried, "don't you dare—"

"I have to, Leda. A few things happened that I can't explain yet. Tipa saved me and I'm a living amulet of god magic and I have an idea."

Her expression revolved through shock, horror, disbelief, and finally, consternation. "A living amulet? This is . . . I just . . . Trust *you* to break the mold," she cried, her voice a little too high.

Unable to help it, I laughed. "Trust me. I've got this."

"What are you going to do?"

"Distract the demigods, of course. Buy Tipa some time."

"You can't sacrifice yourself, B."

"Do you see another option? Ignis and his children are here. They will want me more than anything once they know what I am. They'll do anything. It's an easy distraction. I don't know what Tipa has planned, but it's got to be better than ours."

She opened her mouth, then shut it again. After several moments passed, she let out a frustrated breath, nostrils flared.

"What? How do you know? A living . . . Never mind. We *will* discuss this later."

I stepped closer and grabbed her arms. "This is where you have to trust me, Leda. If we're going to be a Sisterhood, we need to be in this together."

She hesitated again before finally growling, "Fine. You

know that I trust you, but you can't go alone, Bianca. If this is to be a Sisterhood, you have to let me help. We're in this together."

I blinked, startled by her firm tone.

"What if Scarlett needs you?"

A troubled expression crossed her face. Her gaze darted back toward Papa's office, then to me.

"If your father is about to do what I think he's going to do, then I have a feeling Scarlett will be occupied for a little while. Your work is more to the goal of saving the immediate needs of the Network anyway."

Thoughts of Papa's plan lingered in my mind, but I shoved them back. I couldn't worry about that right now. My trust in Papa was complete. He'd do the right thing, whatever that was.

"You really want to be part of this after what happened at the Golden Guinea Hen?" I whispered.

She tilted her head back. "You know that I do. I certainly wouldn't be here now if I didn't, nor volunteering to be with you when this happens. We've fought one war together, Bianca. I'd really like to prevent another one."

Had it been any witch but Leda, I would have thrown my arms around her. With her haughty imperiousness holding her up in a moment of vulnerability, however, I gave her my brightest smile.

Her lips twitched. "Now," she murmured, "shall we go?"

"First, I have something I need to do, and something *you* need to do. Here's my plan."

Chapter Nineteen

The main office for the *Chatham Chatterer* was nestled in the heart of Chatham City.

I transported right outside its main door and peered down the dark road. In the distance, chaos unfurled through sound. Screams. Sobs. Terrified cries. A few shouts as someone directed another witch to go a different way, and then a strange silence. The lack of candles, torches, and general bustle felt worse than the vibrant fear in the air.

Were the demigods sowing chaos to scare witches? To create distractions?

For a moment, I paused to listen.

Nothing.

Shaking my head, I pulled the hood farther over my face and rapped my knuckles on the door to the *Chatham Chatterer*. With the world crumbling outside, there was one place I could rely on witches being busy.

The newsscroll office.

Instead of waiting for someone to admit me, I pressed inside.

A room that smelled like ink and paper greeted me. Two

candles flickered on a desk that looked like it usually housed a witch meant to greet newcomers. Behind that, a curtain that stretched all the way from wall to wall hid the back from me. Darkness coated the front, and only the gentle glow of a candle behind the drapes cast any light.

A low, muttering voice met my ears.

"Merry meet?" I called.

"Go away," barked a woman.

I slipped around the desk and toward the curtain near the right edge. The way her voice echoed around the walls suggested a mostly-open space. The way the furniture laid out naturally led people to the left.

"I'm not here to ask about the demigods," I called.

"I don't care."

"I'm not here to report any information, either."

"Go. Away."

I hedged my way to the right, creeping softly on the balls of my feet. The whisper of my cloak as I slipped toward the wall sounded like explosions in the stillness.

Behind the curtain, the candle snuffed out. I paused. A shadow moved out of the corner of my eye and I ducked. Something heavy slammed into the wall behind me with a thud and the splinter of wood. I reached up, shoved it back, and pushed the witch off-balance. As she stumbled, I gained my feet, grabbed the club—a glassless lamp—and yanked it free.

"What are you doing?" I cried.

"Defending myself!"

"I'm not here to hurt you."

"Right," the witch snapped. "You're just creeping around this place to get something to eat. You might be a demigod for all I know!"

I set the lamp behind me. With a spell, I brought a nearby

candle to life. "No, I'm not a demigod. I do, however, need your help."

A middle-aged woman glared at me from the darkness. Dark hair with streaks of gray framed a heart-shaped face and broad nose, snarling with an upper lip curled back. Tiny, curled parchments dotted the space around her. She plucked each one out of the air and into her palm without breaking eye contact with me.

With both hands lifted up, I slowly moved the hood off my face. Her growl turned to a light gasp when she saw my face.

"What are *you* doing here?" she cried.

"I have a favor to ask."

Five more messages appeared. News reports, I'd wager, from contacts in different parts of the Network. She swiped all of the messages in one hand with a little hiss.

"Get out of my office."

"No."

"I don't need a liability here. Not tonight. The world is starting to unwind at the seams and I don't have time to deal with the High Priest's daughter. Nor all the trouble you seem to escort into Alkarra." She jabbed a hand outside as the sound of a scream sounded in the alley. "Case in point! This all probably started with you!"

"Not even if I'm here to stop the end of Alkarra?"

She hesitated, eyeing me. "You're using this as an opportunity to boost your Sisterhood? Is that what's going on?"

I raised my brow, shocked.

She nodded, eyes wide with a *oh-yes-I-know-about-that-little-secret.*

Before I could ask how, she rolled her eyes. "Don't ask how I know. We pay *very* well for information."

As she spoke, another seven messages found their way in front of her.

"This isn't about the Sisterhood," I said. "This is about the god magic still inside me and how I can help to stop the demigods from taking over."

She froze. "God magic inside you?"

I nodded.

Her expression remained blank for a moment before she lifted an eyebrow in a wordless request to continue.

"I'm an amulet for god magic," I said. "I don't know the details to explain it, but somewhere in the course of me losing goddess magic, gaining god magic, and getting goddess magic back, I've become a living amulet of god magic. It's information I plan to use to stop what's happening, and I need your help."

The woman blinked several times. Her shoulders drew back as she straightened, pulled in a deep breath, and motioned me to the back.

"Come on, then."

* * *

She led me into the back, where movable curtains separated the room into different work areas, all cluttered with desks, shelves with tiny slots for hundreds of scrolls, books overflowing with papers, and so much ink they could have made a lake. Candles flared back to life as we strode to the back.

A long, narrow desk commandeered the space. Scraps of paper filled the entirety of the wooden wall behind it, appearing pasted on. The woman pulled the received messages out of her pockets, muttered an incantation, and tossed them with a fling of her hand. They scattered, pasting themselves to the wooden boards in different groups.

Above each group, a paper with a location written on it organized each one.

The Southern Covens.

Ashleigh.

Hansham.

Eastern Network.

The wall housed all the messages she'd plucked out of the air and then some. I blinked, shocked. There must be at least 10,000 of the little papers. They moved, organizing themselves as more arrived. When two more papers appeared, she smacked them with the back of her hand and they collided with the wall in different places.

"I'm Valera," she said distractedly, "the editor-in-chief of the *Chatham Chatterer* and, for tonight, the only journalist covering what's unfolding. At least from the office. I can't find a couple of my field journalists, but they're always a bit wild when a story is out."

"Nice to meet you Valera."

She eyed me as she lowered into the wooden chair behind her desk and murmured, "Wish I could say the same. What do you want? Of all places you could be tonight, this is probably the last place I would have expected you."

I pulled a parchment from my pocket and extended it to her. "I want you to publish this immediately. Front page head-line. Boldest you can get."

With a sigh, she unrolled it and skimmed the words. Her sharp gaze darted to me, then back to the page. Finally, she lowered into her desk, crossed her hands over each other, and eyed me.

"Why?"

"The only way we're going to win against the demigods is to outwit them. This is my first step toward that end. At least, it'll be a distraction while we round up the remaining leaders we have left in the Network and . . . my friend takes care of a few things."

She motioned to the paper. "Is what you wrote here true?"

"All of it."

"Then how will *this* outwit them?"

"It's too complicated to explain in detail, but I have a plan and it's a better plan than what anyone else will be able to execute."

She scoffed. "You might be his daughter, but you're no Derek Black."

My fingers curled into my fist. "No," I whispered. "I'm not. And that is why this is going to work."

Something in my steady tone seemed to catch her attention. She tilted her head to the side, regarded me, and finally leaned forward.

"I have at least two hundred potential headlines, all of them as important and explosive as this. More so, if we're talking about a public safety concern. Why should I stop telling witches to hide in their homes and defend themselves at all costs for this?"

"Twenty minutes," I said. "Put it on top, bolded, for twenty minutes. Then you can bump it down the scroll. All I need is for the demigods to see it."

"How will they find you?"

"There are clear instructions in there."

She rolled her eyes, then sighed. "And what is to stop Derek Black himself from coming after me once this has all settled down? Plastering his daughter all over the front page in a beckoning call for demigods isn't exactly subtle. I'd rather not get put in the dungeons, thanks."

"If he's still in power?" I murmured, and her eyes glittered with sudden curiosity, "I will vow your protection myself. Papa never acts rashly, Valera. He knows his daughter and that I, alone, hold responsibility for my actions."

"Fine." She stood up. "I'll give it twenty minutes. It will go live in seven."

"Thank you."

She cast me a stern glare. "This is business, Bianca. Not

pleasure. Don't think you're going to exact such a thing without a cost. When the dust settles, you and I will have a nice long talk."

I licked my lips, my hesitation palpable. Did I want to make such a promise to a witch like her? On a scale of powerful witches in the Central Network, the editor-in-chief of the *Chatham Chatterer* was up there next to Baxter. Some of them had been acclaimed as near-political figures, as influential in opinion as Council Members, and far more aware of the Network than most Coven Leaders.

"I promise," I said.

With a nod, she lowered back down to her desk. I turned to go, then stopped. "The last line, about my cottage in Letum Wood?"

"Yes?"

"Make sure that's in there. They need to find me, and fast. Emphasize that I have more power than any amulet. It's the most important part of the piece, next to me being an amulet for god magic."

She paused. "You realize that other witches in the Network will read this? Everything will change for you once this is published, rise of the demigods or not."

"I understand."

Valera blinked, pulled in a deep breath, and said, "Anything else?"

I shook my head.

"So mote it be," she murmured.

I transported away.

* * *

Ten minutes later, I stood inside my cottage.

The Volare lay under my bed, locked safely in its case. I didn't want to take it and risk the demigods unraveling it—if such a thing was possible. Volares had protections against goddess spells or fire or time or unraveling, but god magic might pose another hazard.

Without the Volare or Viveet, I felt more naked than ever.

A lone candle on the table illuminated the room. I lit several more the moment I finished writing a note. The square of paper whispered as it disappeared in a transportation spell, sent to Nicholas and Michelle.

I hoped they were awake.

As calmly as I could, I stood and peered outside. A sound to the left caught my attention. Two figures transported outside my cottage, a few paces away from my front door. Candles in the window flared to life at my command seconds before I opened the door. Leda's white-blonde hair stood there. At her side, a familiar head of variegated hair followed.

"Ava?" I hissed to Leda. "I didn't tell you to bring her!"

Leda scowled. "She threatened to come on her own if I didn't bring her!" she quietly cried. "She said she'd run through the forest and you know she would! She wants to help. She was with Baxter. Two other women arrived to speak with him. His sisters, I think. I took Ava so he didn't have to worry about her. They left."

With any luck, Baxter would be fighting the demigods with Tipa by now.

"*Monilay mal* are here," Ava cried. "I help you! I speak with them. I tell you more. Please, I stay."

My nostrils flared, but we didn't have time to come up with another plan. The demigods would be here soon.

"Get inside," I murmured. "We can't discuss it out here."

Leda ducked into the cottage and Ava followed. I closed the door, bolting it, even though it soon wouldn't matter. The warm light of a fire starting in the hearth gave a surreal sense to my humming heart. This would have felt so normal had doom not rained over all of Alkarra.

"They're in all of the Networks," Leda said, grim. She spoke with measured speed to give Ava time to comprehend. "No one is sure if they're killing our leaders, taking them hostage, or returning to Alaysia with them."

"What do you think, Ava?" I asked.

Ava frowned. "I don't know. It is . . ." She put a hand on her head, indicating confusion.

Leda turned to Ava. "You don't leave my side, you understand? Bianca's magic won't work if the demigods show up, which means she can't protect you." She shot me a long look, then added in a mutter, "she'll barely be able to protect herself."

The trees caught my attention, frantic outside.

The unknown are coming.

The darkness returns.

"They're here," I murmured.

Leda's face paled. "Are you sure about this?" she whispered.

I turned away from Leda to peer outside, where I could sense shapes shifting in the darkness. The candles inside my house burned brightly, creating a barrier to whatever happened outside. Though I couldn't see, I could feel it.

We were surrounded.

"I've never been so sure in my life," I said lightly. "Tonight, we do what the Sisterhood does best."

"What's that?" she whispered.

"Surprise *everyone*," I murmured. I wrapped her in a quick hug, no-touch rules set aside, and she put her hands on my back. After a firm squeeze, I pulled away with a smile. "Go, Leda. You know what to do. I'll see you back at the castle as soon as I can."

Leda sighed. "Then good luck. We'll be in position."

Renewed cries from the trees preceded Leda and Ava scurrying into another transportation spell.

They are here.
The darkness has returned.
It is not right!
We will protect her.

I grabbed an iron poker from my hearth, the hiss of metal on stone a welcome sound. Cold, snowy air met me as I stepped outside. A breeze blew my hair off my cheeks, cooling the flushed skin.

Sometimes, getting out of the cottage helped me hear the smaller voices of the trees. The ones that weren't quite so loud but gave better details. Forcing myself to concentrate, I pressed a hand to a nearby trunk.

Amidst the panic, quieter voices became apparent.

They are here.
We will protect her.

Trees began to shift, moving through the dirt. I'd seen this before. When perceived danger came my way, they'd rearrange themselves into a protective line around my cottage. Trunks scooted against each other, branches tangled, making passage impossible.

My gut twisted inside me in a shot of nerves. No going back now. "I hope this works," I murmured, and crouched down. My fingers burrowed through the icy snow and down to the dirt. Once I touched it, the quality of their voices increased.

"Let them come," I whispered.

The trees quieted slightly. In the background, several more spoke, but they were too far away to hear my voice. News seemed to travel through the forest, as if it could conduct through the root network. After a few more seconds, the trees quieted even further. The shifting branches slowed to allow me to speak clearly again.

"Let the demigods come."

Something filled the air. Hesitation. Tension. As if the

thoughts of the trees could change Letum Wood itself. I looked up as a tree shivered, raining a fall of snow on my shoulders.

"Let them come."

I straightened, snow blowing in my face as an inferno of god magic consumed my body. Shadows appeared in the trees. The crunch of snow beneath boots came next. I lifted the poker and braced myself when a familiar-enough outline appeared in the trees.

Bram strolled down the path.

Chapter Twenty

Well, if this wasn't my worst nightmare come to life.

My fingers tightened around the poker as I drew it into a fighting stance, my legs braced beneath me.

I gritted my teeth, sickened at the sight of him. At the time of Bram's capture, Baxter had had enough confidence in the Court of the Gods that we went along with his plan to send Bram back, though several of us didn't like it. What choice did we have?

Foolish mistake.

A fire-red amulet swayed around Bram's neck as he stopped and gazed around. Eventually, his attention landed on me. He stacked his hands on his hips, regarding me through glittering eyes.

Of course Bram would be here, undoubtedly the leader. In the back of my mind, the trees continued to screech with equal parts panic and fear. I tucked them out of my thoughts, somehow able to bundle them back so they didn't distract me.

"Ah," he drawled, "so there you are."

Images of Igor, the Southern Network High Priest, interplayed over this demigod. I expected the accent from the South, with their inability to pronounce w's and crisp intonations. No such accent came. His natural demigod voice had an annoying length to it, as if he had to draw out all the things he said.

His crimson amulet glittered on his chest, an obnoxious stone that swung from a long chain made out of a metal that I'd seen before. The filigreed edges of the amulet formed a diamond, multifaceted, just like the one I'd broken. Orange pulsed inside. For some reason, it felt like a statement of war.

If I hadn't known any better, I would have thought that this new amulet was actually the one I'd destroyed, Luppentonisa. Darkness had slowly overtaken Luppentonisa until it began to crumble to char. Baxter had taken it back to Alaysia, and I hadn't thought twice about it.

Ignis, clearly, had replaced it.

Or resurrected it.

"Bram." I brought the poker up higher. "Lovely to see you. Welcome to my home. Next time, please let me know in advance of your visit and I'll make a cake. It's poor etiquette over here in Alkarra to just drop in and kidnap our leaders. Not sure how that works in Alaysia."

He frowned. "It's not lovely to see you."

"No?"

He rolled his eyes.

"We don't really like you over here either," I murmured.

At that, he laughed, but the humor quickly died. He wore a dark gray fur across his shoulders, appearing a bit more lean these days. His beard remained, but the warmth that had once been in Igor's eyes was gone. Behind him lurked two other demigods, their amulets boldly displayed as they stepped into the cottage. Such confidence.

I hoped they choked on it.

"You have called me here," Bram said, "with your little

article. Living amulet? Some of my demigods tell me you tricked them with Nicomedianthekus. Clever, I must say. Those same demigods suspected your article was a lie, you know. Me? I didn't. Because we know there is something different about you. Besides, there is no way you could trap me here."

He gestured above him, arms outspread, to indicate the forest overhead.

"You think I want to trap you?" I asked.

"I know it. Why else would you share your location?"

"I didn't share anything. Valera did."

He rolled his eyes. "Why do witches care so much about semantics? It doesn't matter. Is it true? Are you a living amulet?"

"Want to hand me your new bauble there and we can test the theory?"

His fingers twitched at his side. Unable to help myself, I smiled. His lips thinned.

"What does it mean?" he snapped. "You, a living amulet."

"That I'm more powerful than you."

He snorted. "You're a child."

"Yet I found you the first time, and brought you to me the second."

A demigod behind him repositioned, fists flexed. Oh, they didn't like the truth.

"Bested by a witch," I murmured, unable to help myself. "Must be the height of embarrassment back in Alaysia. I hear you're kind of a joke there anyway. Former Tester of god magic in new babies, you stole an amulet, came to Alkarra to get some power and prestige, and mucked it up because of one little mortal girl you let slip away. And me, if you want to get detailed, but I'm okay with Ava taking the credit."

His nostrils flared and for a moment I saw exactly how this night could end. With my Network burning in the background and my father about to do something drastic, I couldn't stop myself from taking the few guaranteed hits I'd have on him.

"You know nothing," he breathed, "of Alaysia."

"Thank the good gods. Oh, wait. Should I *not* do that now?"

"Enough," he snapped. "Are you or are you not an amulet? You have power, supposedly. Are you lying?"

My lips twitched. Ah, the golden bait worked after all. He just couldn't resist the idea of more power. A living amulet. God magic in a new and, perhaps, replicable form.

"I will offer my services again, but this is your last chance. Would you like to test it?"

Bram hesitated, eyeing me. Surely, he sensed a trap. I waited for his response.

Finally, he shook his head. "No. I don't believe you."

I shrugged. "Believe what you want, Bram. Facts don't change based on your investment in them."

"It makes no sense," he snapped. "God magic is not given in that way. It sounds like an excuse. A reason to get me here, to distract me. To stop me from the success you see everywhere in Alkarra right now."

"And yet," I drawled, "you came anyway."

His scowl intensified.

My smile brightened. I pointed the poker at him.

"You don't want to leave unless you know for certain, right? Because you could be walking away from an amulet more powerful than any other. Or, it could be nothing." I lifted my eyebrows, my voice a singsong. "What are you gonna do now, Bram?"

Bram folded his arms across his chest, regarding me through narrowed eyes. A battle waged in his mind, I could see it. He wanted to talk to me, to find out more about my nature, but he wanted to do it on *his* terms.

Besides, he had Alkarra to take over tonight.

What to do?

Control, for an offensive attack, was imperative. Talking to me here, particularly after being lured by such an article, would potentially be playing into my hands, and he wouldn't like that.

Yet he couldn't resist more power . . .

"It will not be me that tests it," he murmured, "nor me that stays here to be caught in your witchy traps. We will be gone from this place and you will see."

My gaze darted to the side, where a flare of fire issued not far away. Several paces from that, another. Overhead came a loud screech at the tops of the trees, then the cracking sound of breaking branches as something heavy dropped through the canopy.

One of the demigods muttered something in another language, then stepped to the side. A clinking sound followed.

Bram narrowed his gaze on me. "Dragons?" he hissed.

I smiled.

"If you think they hate witches, just wait until they encounter an amulet of god magic. They're *really* nasty then."

"You may set me up, little witch, to try to get another amulet, but it will not work this time!" he screeched. "I have learned my lesson."

"But have you?"

The roar of a dragon sounded overhead moments before the ground shook. Fire, tainted with a bright, vibrant purple hue, illuminated the darkness over my house. Five answering roars came next. A sudden increase in emotion from the forest momentarily drew my mind back to the trees.

They fear, the trees whispered, *they fear.*

They run.

They fear.

The cacophony bounced around my mind as I understood

what they tried to say. Bram and the other demigods were afraid.

Of what?

Not the dragons. No, Bram could dispatch them in moments if he wanted to—at least, that's what I assumed. If thought magic was so instantaneous and powerful, what could stop him?

The answer to my question came in his wary gaze as he regarded *me*, not the dragons. While the dragons stomped around outside, Leda and Ava hid back in the bushes. Leda's spells made bushes dance and voices call as if Guardians surrounded my house.

Bram didn't move.

Just to prove my theory, I quickly advanced three steps toward him. The unexpected movement startled him. He threw his hands up, stepping back just as fast.

He growled.

"We will verify this," he cried, "then we will have your story. Take her," he bellowed. "And the others outside, lurking beyond the house. I can hear them out there. Probably that foul little Ava."

With that command, a demigod whisked me away.

* * *

Darkness surrounded me.

Instead of the warmth of my cottage, I faced an underground cellar. Dingy windows, high up a ceiling only a few paces overhead, showed more darkness outside. I doubted much light would come through their dirty panes.

The place smelled like loam and mold. I wrinkled my nose. The cold air burned my nostrils. My breath billowed in white, ghostly spurts. At least I'd kept my winter cloak on. I drew it closer around me, grateful for the reassuring weight.

Now, I just had to escape before they took me back to Alaysia.

Metal bars separated me from the rest of the cellar. Several cells filled the extra space, the others smaller. Chains dangled from the ceiling, near metal circles and hooks. The dirt floor was hard packed beneath my boots.

Shelves, work tables, and benches occupied the other side in a cluttered array. Wine barrels of various sizes stood along one wall, and half-full wooden buckets filled with apples. Based on the smell of this place, they'd long gone sour.

Stairs created by loose stones and chinked mud flowed up through a hole near the edge of the room. A rudimentary staircase. Most of the stones weren't even, though the tops had been worn almost smooth. It would be treacherous if this place ever became wet. Surely, it did. The walls were dirt, a few roots peeking out of them here and there. I reached to touch one, wondering if it would connect me to the forest.

Nothing.

With a sigh, I backed away from the bars. A wooden chair had been nailed to one wall. I lowered into it. This place could be in the Southern Network, maybe. Or a root cellar in the North? Based on what little I saw, it was impossible to tell.

Heat smoldered through my body, so an amulet must be somewhere nearby. The warmth felt softer, more removed, not as intense as Bram.

I paused, listening.

This wasn't just a root cellar. A scrape of something overhead sounded like a chair. So there was another floor, likely with witches or demigods above. A few quiet murmurs came through the wood, but it was impossible to detect what they said. Based on the tones, it could be *yazika*.

I cast an incantation to amplify the sound, but nothing happened. No stir of goddess magic, even. Just the low, quiet flicker of god magic in my blood. Did the cell have a magical block on it or was it just my wonky goddess magic?

When I felt certain no one would come down to check on me, I closed my eyes. Now, I had to focus on what to do next. Capture had seemed inevitable, though I'd hoped to avoid it.

Now, I had to get *really* clever.

Tipa appeared in my thoughts. What word had she used in regards to god magic?

Oh, right. *Intent.*

Thought magic and intent. With that in mind, I tried to imagine fire in my hands. I pictured the way the flame curled, faded to blue, and white hot in the center. In my mind, I could see the way it danced, bouncing up and down, flopping like it didn't know where it wanted to go. As I pictured a flame, I imagined it on my palm. The heat on my skin.

Nothing happened.

My second attempt, I focused longer. Pictured different sizes of flame. Imagined it on the bench next to me, on the ground, on the stairs. Felt the burn, maybe even the pain. With it, I tried to infuse all my hope and wishing possible. My mind wobbled with whether I pictured the right thing. Was it orange or yellow on top? Blue or white on bottom?

Maybe both?

No fire appeared.

Intent, I thought. *What does that even mean?*

As an amulet *and* a magic holder, logically, I should be able to use the god magic within me. Except god magic rarely made sense. Hadn't Tipa stated that also? Although, really, none of this made sense. That I had god magic in me at all didn't come together with logic or facts. It shouldn't be there.

Half an hour or so later, I was no further along. A headache knotted the back of my neck, but I ignored it. Frantic now, I attempted to use god magic to make something else happen. Anything.

Nothing worked.

A door slammed open. Light spilled into the cellar before a heavy thud of boots, scattering rocks, and a torch.

With a sharp breath, I focused on the heat in my blood and tried to pull from it. Move a barrel of wine. Sort rotting apples. Despite my desperation to prove it, nothing worked. Bram stepped off the stairs and stood in front of me.

I rose to my feet and forced my racing heart to calm.

"Merry meet," he murmured, eyes bright. "Goddess magic is suppressed here—you won't be able to escape. The only way to open this cell is through my magic. Did you see there was no door? I would have to use god magic to send these bars away. We are far from your home, far from your witches, and far from anything you know. Will you be so brave without your dragons and your forest?"

"You're right," I said, aghast. "I've forgotten my manners. Did you worry I wouldn't thank you?" I gestured around me. "The accommodations are . . . lovely."

He ignored me to pace back and forth across the basement floor. "Are you a living amulet?"

"Presumably."

"Then we shall find out, won't we? You touch another amulet and it dies, then it's true. Amulets cannot touch each other. This you know?"

I rolled my eyes, as if he insulted me.

In fact, I hadn't known.

He scowled, but didn't face me directly. Several pairs of feet came down the stairs. These were halting, almost . . . reluctant. A female demigod spilled into the space near Bram, followed by two others. They held both arms behind her back. She eyed me with fury.

Tipa.

My stomach clenched. Uh oh. The wrath in her expression would have cleaved me in half if it hadn't been swamped by a hearty measure of fear. She widened her eyes as if to ask *what have you done?*

"Jikes," I whispered.

Had Bram taken her hostage? If so, then why hadn't he taken her amulet? Why didn't she just disappear? A dozen more questions sped through my mind, but they faded back when Bram slammed Tipa into the bars and shouted, "Give her your amulet!"

Tipa put her hands up at the last second, sparing her face from being shoved into metal. I stepped back, out of her reach.

Tipa met my gaze, but spoke to Bram.

"No."

Bram snarled.

Tipa's voice filled my mind.

Intention, she hissed, clearly using god magic to speak to me. *Use your intent to see the result happen. Don't just think about it or hope it. Intend for your end state to be* true. *Make it be so by the power of your desire.*

My voice trembled when I said, "I don't know what will happen if you give the amulet to me."

Magic kept her pressed to the bars, struggling to take a deep breath. She frowned, then tried to look back over her shoulder to Bram. He hovered away from the cage, as if disgusted.

She grunted, nostrils flared, and tried to wiggle free to no avail. The two demigods that escorted her down stood as far away as possible. They didn't want to be anywhere near me when it happened.

"Do it," Bram hissed, moving his amulet on the chain so it hung behind his back. "Now!"

Her eyes widened at me, as if to say *try already!* I regarded her for a full breath before the puzzle clicked into place.

"She's a servant of Deasylva," Tipa called. "Do you want to anger the goddesses?"

A distraction, surely. She was buying me time to try god magic.

Bram growled a response, but I didn't hear. My thoughts barreled away from me, racing toward god magic and intent. Because *thought* and *intent* were two very different things.

Thinking one thing into being would create chaos in any magic system. An errant thought, out-of-control of our conscious mind, would cause all manner of things to spontaneously occur. Chaos would be a strong tenant of such an easily-accessed magic, so the gods would have had to have one way to control it.

To harness it.

Thoughts coupled with *intent* meant a desire, however. Purpose. You could think of an intention as quickly as a thought, but you wouldn't *intend* to do something as errantly. There would be a motivation behind it.

Intention meant control. It gave structure to the magic.

With a sharp breath, I pictured Tipa setting the amulet in my hand, but the amulet never touching my skin. Instead, it hovered above my palm. While there, darkness would cloud the amulet. Not real, of course, just an illusion.

Bram hissed at me.

"Move forward!" he shouted.

I stood there, torn. The magic brightened in my belly, hot and powerful. It hadn't felt like this before. My motivation for this outcome was even greater than my thoughts. I didn't want to destroy her amulet, her access to home, to help. I wanted Tipa to break free as much as I wanted to fool Bram.

"No," I whispered.

Then I pictured exactly how I'd make that happen.

A murderous growl followed from Bram. I hovered out of reach until I couldn't anymore. Bram used magic to shove me forward. I put my hands up to avoid slamming into the bars, just like Tipa.

Bram instantly shuffled back, body canted to the side, a grimace on his face. I held out my hand, much lower than hers.

Tipa met my gaze.

With my left eye, I gave half a wink. She paused, then dropped the amulet into my palm.

God magic bloomed through my blood as I saw my goal through. The amulet fell to my palm, but never touched it. It hung just above the skin.

Instantly, a black film overcame half of her amulet. It cracked in the middle, a deep ravine of black. For good luck, I brought a little smoke into place to see the illusion all the way through. The smell of char followed next. All of it to convince Bram of his worst nightmare.

The scene unfolded before my eyes.

Tipa reeled back with a cry. Darkness stained the front of the amulet, spreading slowly. The smoke ebbed a little. Bram stared at it, eyes wide and pale. He looked from the amulet, to me, then back again. I didn't move my hand, just stared at the gem. Heat raced around me in giddy whirls, as if pleased to finally be used.

"The gods," Bram muttered, his voice hoarse. "She *is* the amulet-breaker."

I lifted my hand and the amulet followed, always a hint above the skin, and dumped it back into her hand.

"Sorry," I whispered.

The darkness and smoke remained in place as she closed her fingers over it. Confusion registered on her face next. Could she tell it was fake? Did she still feel the power of the amulet? I stood there, impassive.

The horror of her gaze faded into something like a question. With a single, subtle back and forth just once, I said *no*. A hopeful sign that she'd understand. At the last second, she turned back to her amulet and screamed.

Words in a different language poured out of her. The other demigods came to life with horror. They scrambled to get away, running upstairs. All of them faded, disappearing out of the cellar except for Bram.

He eyed me with a bright smile.

"A living amulet indeed," he murmured. "You are now mine. When I am done dealing with your father, you will go to the Courts of the Gods, my dear. Ignis, god of fire, will question you next."

Chapter Twenty-One

My mind whirled in the aftermath.

Alone in the cellar, I blinked and looked at my hands. I'd done it. Somehow, I'd used god magic and it had been . . . easy. Once I'd figured it out, at least. Bram didn't seem to suspect, either.

Yet.

The silence seemed so loud, banging in my ears with my heart. The god magic still whirled warmly inside my blood.

Questions followed. Had *I* become Luppentonisa? Would Bram be able to use me as an amulet? I shook the question away. Those could come later. For now, I had a new power at my disposal.

Intention.

God magic.

Everything Tipa told me whirred through my mind until I let the thoughts settle, one by one.

Overwhelmed, I faded back from the bars and lowered onto the wood chair. My cloak kept the bitter cold out as I pulled my knees to my chest and let myself think it through. I willed the bars to disappear and pictured myself walking out of the cellar to save my father.

The bars faded from around me.

My breath hitched.

Could magic be that easy?

I paused, waiting for Bram to storm back down and haul me off to Alaysia. Whether it was my split concentration, hesitation, or something else, the bars reappeared. I frowned and tried again, but they flickered, remaining. When I reached out, they felt cool on my fingertips.

Could god magic be countered? Would Bram feel me remove his god magic? I doubted it. It didn't seem like a type of magic that created ties or awareness, but I didn't know for sure. My knowledge resembled a thin, translucent layer of ice on top of an entire ocean. Unfortunately, I needed to walk across that ice and save my father, my Network.

My thoughts stumbled over themselves for several more minutes before my body began to calm. Deep breathing, intentional reviewing, and murmuring the facts to myself calmed my runaway heart. It reoriented me into the moment, away from the questions, and helped me focus again.

Perhaps removing Bram's magic wasn't the path.

Maybe taking myself *out* of his magic was.

I willed myself to appear on the other side of the bars, and . . . a second later I stood there.

The instantaneous change felt too simple. I glanced around, waiting for a demigod to pounce out of the shadows.

No, they wouldn't come back here. At least I'd done that much correctly. They thought I was a plague and, except for Tipa, certainly hadn't considered that I might *use* the magic. My heart thumped as I pictured myself writing a letter to Leda, a quill and pen appearing in front of me. A letter. I would write her a letter and explain—

The quill and paper appeared.

Hands shaking, I reached out to touch the parchment. It hovered in the air, giving way under my fingertips. Before they disappeared, I grabbed them. Maybe god magic was more impermanent. If not used right away, did it fade like our thoughts, our intent?

Noise overhead drew my gaze up and I held my breath. Someone walked across the floor upstairs, causing dust to trickle near my face. I let the breath out when they didn't open the door, Bram's promise about Papa ringing through my mind.

When I am done dealing with your father.
Quickly, I scrawled a note.

Change of plans. Meet me outside Papa's apartment as soon as you can.

Bring Ava.

—B

With a fluttering heart, I knew that Leda would receive it and open it immediately. It would find her where she stood.

The letter disappeared.

As I turned to glance upstairs, wondering if it would really be as simple as leaving, a shuffle of sound sent my heart into a tizzy.

I whirled around, reaching uselessly to my waist, and gasped. A slight male witch appeared a few paces away, blinking.

His thin eyes, slanted slightly at the edges, and lean frame made me think he was a Southern Network witch. He had dark hair, scuffed to the side, the length of his ears. He wore the seal-skin boots of the lowest clans in the South, the ones who lived on the disappearing sea, near what most considered the end of the world.

This witch regarded me, then held two hands up, showing me his palms in a gesture of peace. The lack of heat told me he'd just arrived with goddess magic.

My gaze narrowed.

"Who are you?" I whispered in Yazika.

He jerked his head to the left, a silent way of saying *no* in the Southern Network clans. His gaze darted around, breath coming fast, as if he'd been running. One breath at a time, he calmed.

With a heavy swallow and a wary eye on me, he reached behind him with one hand and fiddled around for a moment. A piece of twine wrapped around his chest loosened. When he brought his arm back around, a long object wrapped in fur lay in his hand. I watched him warily. With both hands he held onto the object. A flick of his wrist moved reindeer fur away. A sword appeared there, nestled in the folds.

I sucked in a sharp breath.

"Viveet."

Her silver appearance gleamed despite the dim light, as if she shone from within. Gentle blue strands of ivy illuminated the length of the sword, smoldering a dark sapphire.

"Andrei?" I gasped.

He hesitated, then jerked his head to the right. Yes.

"Viveet," he whispered haltingly in the common tongue. "She bring me to you. She want you back. Now. Impatient."

"You have magic?"

Andrei nodded, then lifted Viveet closer. "You need," he whispered. "You need now. Demigods here. You need."

"How?" I whispered. "How did you get your magic back?"

He jerked his head to the left.

"No time."

My heart hiccuped as I studied my sword. She appeared exactly the same. The familiar hilt. Blue flame. Etched ivy patterns extended along her blade in the pattern from before. Even the sweeping *A* had been replaced in the blade, near the bottom.

He turned his wrist, released the hilt, and extended Viveet to me. His strong fingers handled her like a natural.

"Whole again," he whispered.

Tears welled up in my eyes as I wrapped my fingers around her hilt. Blue light sped through the ivy pattern in a spray of sparks, then flames that exploded in the air with a crackle.

Andrei ducked back, grinning.

Power moved all the way from my fingertips, through my shoulder, into my heart. I gasped, thrilled and empowered. The same energy I felt the first time I touched Viveet returned to me now, only more powerful than ever. God magic swirled with it, tangibly hot, irritated by the burst of goddess magic in my hands.

"Viveet," I whispered, my voice thick.

The blue flames brightened, as if to say *merry meet*. I studied her, hefted her. Twirled her back, brought her into guard, and sent her through the air. Each movement, a dance. Each thrust felt like coming home.

It *was* Viveet.

The exact length, weight, and balance. Every part of her hummed, buzzing in me. I lowered her, my fingers tight around her hilt. Her light dropped from a bright flame to a quiet, moving blue.

"Stop bad demigods," he murmured. "Viveet is strong. Made for this."

I rubbed Viveet's hilt with my thumb.

"I will. Thank you, Andrei, for my sword."

He nodded to Viveet. "Both whole now. You and me? We

all fight." Both of his hands went to his chest, then he bowed at the waist. He transported away with a whisper of sound.

Viveet's glowing, happy metal pulsed bright in my hands. Whole. Ready. Not a trace of breakage within her. With god magic, I brought the Volare. Viveet's old sheath came with it.

My magical rug spun around me in a dizzying spiral, then rolled up, slipped into the case, and flung itself over my shoulder. I buckled the sheath.

Breathing hard, I blinked back happy tears. Now the Sisterhood had finally come together.

Bianca Monroe was back.

Chapter Twenty-Two

A breath later, I appeared at Chatham Castle.

Viveet hung in her sheath at my left hip, right where she belonged. Her weight sent joy flying through me, warm as god magic and twice as potent. The Volare bumped on my back, rattling in the carrier, as if it couldn't contain its own happiness.

Leda and Ava waited for me in the hall, a few paces away from Papa's apartment, as if they'd just arrived. Leda looked at me, then Viveet, then back. Her eyes widened, large as globes.

"What," she whispered, "happened? We heard Bram arrive, and we were able to do everything you told us in the bushes. They almost got us, but Ava bit one of them. I was able to pull her away and transport."

"Long story. I'll tell you later," I said quickly, "we need to stop Bram right now. I think he's probably wherever my father is."

"His office."

"We'll check there first. Did you find Sanako?"

Leda nodded. "She's on her way. She had to find whatever you requested from her first."

"Where will she meet you?"

"I'll send her a message to tell her your father's office."

While she used a spell to summon a piece of parchment and a quill, I looked at Ava. "Will it hurt you if I use god magic to make you invisible?"

Her eyes widened. "God magic? You?"

I nodded. She hesitated, then swallowed. "Little pain, not big. But it's okay. I be there!" she added, seeing my doubt.

Finally, I said, "All right, but tell me if it's too much."

Her face hardened into steel.

Leda nodded as the note to Sanako faded in a flutter. "The plan is ready," she murmured.

"Then let's go."

* * *

When I pressed the shell of my ear to Papa's door, not a sound slipped through.

I didn't doubt that someone had cast a silencing incantation to keep everything inside. No Protectors lurked in the hallway, but they wouldn't. Certainly not visibly, anyway. They were likely attempting to recover Council Members and help the Network.

"I can take you both in there with god magic. I think it's safe to do so. Both magicks are inside me, and we know that Priscilla touched Baxter's amulet without losing her magic. If you don't want to risk it, however, then you don't have to."

Leda shook her head. "God magic. Jikes, Bianca. Of course I trust you."

I reached for Ava's hand. She slipped cold, shaky fingers into mine. I gave her a reassuring squeeze, then with another stir of god magic, I pressed all of us into invisibility. Leda sucked in a breath.

"You all right?" I murmured.

"Surprisingly, yes. But it's . . . weird."

"Ava?"

Her voice sounded a bit thin, but strong. "Fine."

"Then let's go."

The next thing I knew, we stood in Papa's office, entering right into a scene of chaos and tension unlike any I'd known before.

Bram stood in the middle of the room. Council Member Aldred, Matthias, and Baxter hovered in the air, bound with ropes. They seemed unable to move, locked into position with contorted expressions of pain. The flare of heat that rippled through my blood almost robbed my concentration and revealed us.

Bram used so much power. Did his magic fight with Baxter's? How many amulets were in this room?

Baxter's wristguard amulet lay on the ground in front of Bram. It was unlikely that Bram came here alone, so I'd have to presume that other demigods were invisible. We ran a veritable risk of bumping into someone that we couldn't see with every step we took. It would reveal us, and remaining out of sight was key.

"Don't move," I murmured to Leda. "Stay here against the wall with Ava." I paused, then added, "When Sanako arrives, let her in. Somehow."

"I will," she breathed. "I'll figure it out."

"The time of the witches has passed," Bram shouted, drawing my gaze. "The time of the demigods has come. You, Highest Witch of the most powerful Network, will not stand in our way. After years of time in Alaysia, we have *earned* Alkarra."

Papa stood behind his desk, face etched with rage. "Joke's on you, Bram. I'm not the Highest Witch anymore."

A gasp rippled through the witches in the room.

Papa charged.

He knocked into Bram's midsection with a hard slam. My heart jumped into my throat. How had he been able to hit Bram? Bram should have moved himself with a thought, but he didn't.

Bram shoved Papa back and Papa flew across the room. A moment before he slammed into his desk, a shield sandwiched itself between his back and the desk. He hit it with a grunt. The wood splintered beneath the shield, but didn't break.

Papa leapt back to his feet, legs braced.

As Bram straightened, his face contorted in a snarl. His amulet glowed, so bright it was difficult to look at.

Another plan populated through my mind.

Across the room, Scarlett lingered back in the shadows, near Marten, Niko, Alina, and Geralyn. Leda had done her job of gathering the Network leaders well. But where was Lana from the West?

Tension radiated through all of the Network leaders. No doubt Papa tried to send Scarlett out of the way on purpose, but it said something that she hadn't left entirely. If *he* wasn't the Highest Witch, Scarlett was. Her cryptic conversation at my cottage suddenly made a lot more sense.

My throat tightened. Papa was prepared to die tonight. He'd already surrendered, turned the Network over to Scarlett, and now he faced Bram. Bram who, for all intents and purposes, could easily kill Papa.

That thought touched my brain like a wingtip on gentle water, then flew away. I couldn't entertain it. Couldn't afford the distraction.

I had to save Papa, too.

The riotous fire in my body likely meant Bram controlled most of what happened here through his amulet, although I didn't know for sure. Invisible demigods could be holding

Baxter, which would free up Bram. I had my doubts, however. Bram had something to prove. Now more than ever.

Had he come here to usurp Papa on his own? To lay claim to Alkarra without any help? Trust an arrogant demigod.

With god magic still intact, I brought myself to Marten's side, invisible.

"Marten," I whispered, "do you trust me?"

His back straightened. He didn't look away from Papa and Bram grappling yet again, this time whirling around each other. Papa couldn't transport around his office, and Bram seemed unable to do intricate god magic *and* keep the other witches at bay. If Matthias or Baxter entered the fight, Bram would lose. He must know this.

"Bianca?" Marten whispered.

"Do you trust me?"

"Yes."

"Join the fight. Engage Bram. Force him to split his attention. I want him to bind you in the air with the others, but I won't let him kill you."

A thousand questions seemed to spin through Marten's mind, but overflowing out from there was relief. How he could stand to watch his son pit himself against a demigod, I couldn't fathom. I could barely stomach it myself.

Fire exploded behind me as Bram set all the parchments on Papa's desk to flame. Papa recoiled, rolling off before the heat consumed him.

"Gladly," Marten muttered.

In a breath, he charged.

Silently, he threw himself on top of Bram's back. With a roar, Bram grabbed Marten's arm and tossed him into the air. Before Marten landed, he froze into position. Ropes appeared around his arms. He suspended in air, next to a livid Matthias, utterly frozen.

Bram shouted and dropped to his knees. It all but

confirmed my theory that an amulet had limited power. Bram couldn't do everything.

I used the moment of distraction to god magic myself to Papa's side. He stood back, panting, and stared in horror at Marten. Sweat trickled down Papa's face.

"Attack from the right," I hissed. "I'll get his amulet from the left. Keep it open."

Confusion clouded Papa's features, but as I hoped, he didn't take his gaze off Bram. Papa breathed my name, but I had already magicked over near Bram. He struggled to stand from the floor, face twisted in a grimace.

The amulet vibrated on his chest. As I hoped, he'd almost magicked himself out. Just as I reached to snatch the amulet from his front right, he shoved to his feet. The brush of my hand on his arm distracted him. He jerked to the left, gazing through me in confusion.

Papa attacked from the right.

My heart lifted in a moment of hope that Papa would be able to tackle him, and I could wrestle the amulet free, but Bram moved too quickly. He created a wall of ice that crackled as it sprouted from the floor up, blocking Papa. Papa attempted to dispel before he slammed into the crackling sheet, but didn't have the chance. The clear, bluish wall cracked under Papa's weight, but held strong.

Bram whirled around, hand clasping his amulet. His eyes darted around, appearing mad.

"Who was it?" he screeched.

If he could have seen me, he would have stared right into my eyes. The fingers on my left hand wrapped around Viveet. I held my breath.

Shards of skittering ice danced across the floor as Papa broke through the ice wall, sword drawn. With a shout, he fell to his knees, body contorted. The sword clattered to the ground. Papa's fingers tightened, his back writhed as he cried out in pain.

Bram cast a wary gaze around again, then turned to face my father. Just in case, I withdrew Viveet. The hiss of her out of the sheath was almost silent.

"You," Bram panted as he spoke to Papa, "will never defeat me, Derek Black. Never will a witch overpower a demigod again."

Four other demigods materialized, hidden behind Bram in a flanking position, two on each side. They advanced toward Papa. Another demigod had a slash of red across his forehead. A black eye. A roughed-up lip. His curly hair and dark disposition made him stand out from the others. Though I couldn't say why, I had a feeling *that* was Jote.

Which meant Merrick might be here.

A second demigod had almost translucently white skin. His brown hair cut short, with thin shoulders and full lips. An amulet glittered on his left wrist with five red gems. The demigod that Papa had described seeing in the Western Network.

The other two lingered back, teeth bared, gems hidden.

Niko, Geralyn, Alina, and Scarlett met the demigods step-for-step until they circled behind Papa. Niko's upper lip curled over his teeth, his gaze intent on a demigod at the back. Scarlett's chin remained high. Snarling ferocity crackled in the air.

"Derek may not defeat you himself," Scarlett called, "but *we* will defeat you together."

Bram threw out both of his arms, holding the advancing demigods back.

"Do nothing!" he shouted. "Not a move. Alkarra is mine. You will not share my glory with our father!"

He advanced on Scarlett with a shout. A knife materialized in his hands. Behind him, Baxter wavered and nearly dropped to the floor. Viveet flared to life as I used god magic to put myself between Bram and Scarlett.

His knife slammed into Viveet with a flash of blue fire and sparks.

I allowed the god magic to slip back, revealing me. Scarlett gasped.

"Threaten my father," I hissed, "and you threaten me."

Bram shouted. With his distraction, I brought Viveet down, disarming him. Then I used magic to grab his free arm and yank him forward.

Off balance, he stumbled into me. I dropped Viveet, gripped his wrist in both of my hands, and twisted it behind his back. I shoved him down, grabbed the necklace with my right hand and yanked as hard as I could.

The links shattered.

God magic propelled me back on my command. I somersaulted in the air, landing invisibly a few paces away.

The amulet sizzled near my hand, but I touched only the chain. Bram choked, trying to scream. He'd dropped to his hands and knees, a hand outstretched. The four other demigods whirled around, searching for me.

I materialized, holding the amulet up. "Come one step closer," I shouted, "and I'll destroy this one too. You want to be the demigod to tell Ignis you let the amulet-breaker have another one?"

All four of them hesitated.

Behind them, Baxter, Marten, Aldred, and Matthias dropped. Baxter broke the ropes that bound him in a single move and lunged for his wrist guard. Matthias ripped his bonds off, while Aldred panted on the floor, pale. Papa fell onto his back, then swiftly recovered, rolling into a trembling crouch. He grimaced, breathing hard.

The middle demigod I assumed was Jote growled, teeth

bared. His nostrils flared. He advanced a few steps, stopping only when I extended my free hand closer to the amulet.

"What are you going to do, little girl?" he sang. "Break another one?"

Merrick appeared out of nowhere, approaching Jote from behind. He stalked like a panther, silent, with controlled fury in his gaze. I readjusted my hold on the chain. Everything in my body felt hot, overpowered. My skin itched, like lava flowed beneath it.

"Think I might take the power myself," I said to buy time. Merrick had ten paces left before he tackled Jote from behind. "Haven't you heard the news? I'm an amulet too, now. Maybe I'll take *all* the amulets and *all* the god magic to myself. How does that sound?"

"You're nothing against us," Jote hissed.

"Oh really?" I drawled. With more god magic, I sent a spiral of air around Bram. When it faded, he lay on the ground, arms and legs tied, screaming into a mouth gag. My face hardened as I looked back to Jote.

"Try me, demigod."

Merrick threw himself on top of Jote, forcing him to the ground. Matthias followed right behind him, reaching for an amulet around Jote's chest. Seconds later, Matthias held what appeared to be a braided rope with a large, orange bauble on it.

"Got it!" he shouted.

Two demigods sprinted toward me, but a third magicked out of sight. A scream of, "Now!" ripped through the room a second before the third demigod appeared like a battering ram only a pace away from me.

The rest of the witches attacked.

The demigod slammed into me, shoving me with two overly-powerful arms. The force threw me across the room, amulet still in my hands. Papa appeared a second too late, tackling the demigod to the ground.

Moments passed in eternities as I soared over the desk and collided with the glass panes behind it. The glass cracked, giving way on the bottom. It crumbled, spraying into the wintry night in a glittering storm.

I went with it.

A second before I would have fallen into the snowy void below, a pale hand grabbed mine.

"I have you!"

Dangling from Papa's window, I looked up to Leda. Her terrified eyes were wide, shocked. She slipped farther out of the window herself, then cast a spell to glue our hands together. The god magic turned to an inferno inside me. The hand holding the amulet burned. If she let me go, I'd drop. I had too much power now. I couldn't think about anything else.

Another body appeared next to Leda, grabbed my arm, and hauled me up. Sandy blond hair and bright eyes jerked me back into Papa's office. Over the howl of the snow outside, Merrick cried, "Are you all right?"

My back and shoulders ached from slamming into the window, and my whole body felt like it would soon be turned to a crisp, but I nodded.

"Fine," I gasped. "Where's Bram?"

Sanako stood behind Bram, who had been bound by a pair of magic-reinforced manacles he couldn't break. With a spell from Niko, Bram silenced his infernal screaming and stared at the wall, boneless.

Baxter, Papa, Matthias, and Marten grappled with the remaining demigods. Baxter fought one on the ground until Scarlett sent a paralyzing spell. It worked only a few seconds, but enough for Sanako to get a different pair of her father's manacles around his wrists.

With a muttered curse, I shoved the chain into Merrick's hand, gasped "Don't touch the amulet," and hurried over.

Sliding into place while Baxter attempted to wrestle the demigod, I scrambled to find the amulet.

"Ankle!" Baxter gasped.

I reached to the ankle, ripped the amulet off, and scattered back. The amulet felt like cradling a coal. Heat waved through me again. I gasped through it as the demigod roared, furious. Muttering something, Baxter disappeared with him.

"Where's he going?" I cried.

"Dungeons," Marten muttered.

Jote lay unconscious on the ground. I hurried to the next demigod. Niko followed behind me, issuing paralyzing spells for the amulet-less demigods.

While Papa and the final demigod grappled, I came up from behind, magicked a rope onto the demigod's wrist, and yanked him toward me. He shouted, falling to his knees from the force of my pull, and disappeared entirely.

Baxter returned from taking the other demigod to the dungeon. When he reached for Jote, Merrick held up a staying hand. Baxter paused.

Merrick stood over Jote, nudging his face with a boot, until Jote's eyes fluttered back open. Only a second or two passed before he comprehended Merrick's face, then snarled. He lunged, but Sanako's manacles held true. Merrick shoved a boot on Jote's chest and pinned him to the ground.

A hesitation in Jote's reactions likely meant he'd tried to magic away. Frantically, he looked to his chest, then back to Merrick.

Hatred built there.

"You killed my High Priestess," Merrick hissed. "Now she will finally be avenged."

A slam of his fist into Jote's face sent Jote back into unconsciousness. Merrick nodded to Baxter, who grabbed Jote by the arm and hauled him up. They disappeared. Merrick immediately swung around, looking for me.

I stepped back, my body wavering. The room turned hazy. Despite the lessening intensity from the fight, god magic continued to build inside me. Broiling. Hot. Scalding. Too much. My soul burned like hellfire, hot.

A voice filled with power came to me again.

There is much, it whispered, *that we have to say to each other.*

Ignis.

I shuddered, dropping the amulets into distinctly separate places before they burned me from the inside out. Baxter hurried to my side, scooping them up. He put two in separate pockets, a third in the air, and held onto two others. Five amulets.

"I have them," he said quietly.

His arms caught me when I fell, a breath before my head would have banged into the ground. Carefully, he lowered me down.

With the amulets gone, the heat began to fade. Ebbing back, away. My mind scattered. Where was Viveet? The Volare lay firm against my back still. Ava?

Leda?

Cold wind whipped into the room from the broken window. I smelled Letum Wood.

No, Merrick.

Even though the heat ebbed, I felt hollowed out. Hot. Angry. Tired. Papa came up to my side as I used goddess magic to call Viveet to me again. Baxter stepped back, making way for him. Viveet appeared in my hand. Tears filled my eyes. My goddess magic wasn't gone, then. I looked up at Papa.

"You're all right, Papa?"

He pressed a hand to my cheek. "The good gods," he muttered. "You. Are. Crazy."

I chuckled, and he shook his head, muttering threats on my life under his breath. Relief ran through me in bright, delighted waves. Leda appeared at my side, Ava with her, as I slumped against Papa. He leaned into me, breathing heavily.

"We did it," I whispered.

Leda smiled. "We did it," she replied.

I tilted my head back and laughed.

Chapter Twenty-Three

Less than an hour later, almost the entire Central Network Council filled Papa's office.

Scarlett, Marten, and Matthias stood near Papa's desk while they quietly spoke with Aldred and a handful of others. Martha remained missing, but Protectors had been sent in search of her. Xander and Rosanna had been found. They met with apothecaries downstairs. Leda hovered close to Scarlett's side, a bit pale but still on her game.

Niko, his Assistant Hector, and a few other Eastern Network Council Members occupied the right side of the room.

Geralyn's escort—Regina and Merrick included—were on the far side, near the fire. Marten had used a spell to fix Papa's window, and a warm fire danced in the hearth. The High Priestess of the West, Lana, had returned to the Arck and sent a message that indicated she'd arrive in the morning.

Flanked by two protective butlers in a chair by the fire, Alina remained calm and collected as ever.

Ava and Baxter stood near the door, speaking with Tipa, whom Baxter had found after I told him what happened. She gazed my way with deepest annoyance, then left. Soon, I'd thank her, but I had a feeling Tipa and I weren't done with each other yet.

Amidst the collected groups of witches, servants, apothecaries, reporters, and more sashayed in and out of the room. Most of them were stopped by butlers in the hall, but some were allowed through to clean up glass, tend the fire, or pass around warm cups of tea infused with bolstering herbs. One sat in my hand now, steaming.

Merrick stood next to his High Priestess with his arms folded across his chest, a glare on his face that prevented anyone from approaching him. He looked worse than me. Ragged. Exhausted. A split lip on the bottom, scuffed ear, swollen jaw. Even his neck had a scratch running the length of it. Dried blood crusted one nostril, and I thought I saw a gentle shine around his left eye.

A story with Jote and Merrick lingered somewhere in there.

Thankfully, all delegations already agreed to handle the demigod punishment on our own this time. The traitorous gods could get over it.

Jote had been promised to the North, taken away by Masters to suffer death in the morning. Another demigod was taken to La Torra in the Eastern Network to face punishment for crimes in the East—particularly with Niko. The determined set of Niko's face suggested twin levels of relief and despair.

Somewhere, in the chaos, Papa had disappeared.

"You all right, B?" Baxter murmured. He lowered onto the divan next to me, and I felt better with his long body at my side.

"When can I leave?" I asked.

"As soon as Marten says you can," he murmured. "The Council mentioned something about wanting to interview you tonight, but he refused. He's . . . working on it. They're getting up to speed on what your father did."

My throat constricted.

Papa . . . no longer the Highest Witch. The box he'd pulled from his desk had contained none other than the hallowed Esmelda Scrolls. Somehow, he'd transferred his power as Highest Witch to Scarlett, ready to die for his Network.

I could hardly wrap my mind around it. History was replete with High Priests that had been naughty or impractical or genuinely terrible at their job. They had been dealt with through various means, but none of them had been as born for this as Papa.

He'd not only made history by pulling us through Almorran magic, the breaking of borders, and now the incursion of a mortal and demigods. He'd now make it by renouncing the throne, and why? Snatches of conversation drifted through the air. I tuned into them, hopeful for scraps of information.

"The four demigods with Bram were all active in different Networks," murmured someone from the East. "We aren't the only fools here tonight. The demigods have been making politics and issues messy everywhere."

"Derek removed himself as High Priest," old man Halifax said to a newly-arrived Rosanna as he passed a weary hand over his eyes, "appointing Scarlett. Apparently, there is an allowance for such a thing in the Esmelda scrolls. Scarlett said she'll explain everything tomorrow. The Council is having an emergency session in an hour."

Rosanna replied with something I couldn't hear, and didn't try to. The thought of demigods attempting to invade Halifax's house and take him hostage sent a brief smile to my face. Old curmudgeon probably tried to throw his cigar case at them.

I let all the gentle chaos pass through my exhausted mind.

As if he sensed my crumbling, Baxter reached over and put a warm hand on my shoulder. He squeezed. I closed my eyes and longed for sleep.

"Just a few more minutes," he murmured.

Witches peered at me in question, but I ignored them. Niko's gaze wandered to me often, just like Marten. Sometimes Merrick. Questions filled every one of them. Questions I didn't want to answer yet.

Other than Baxter, only Ava approached. Every few minutes, she'd sit by me and rest her head on my shoulder. I'd put my arm around her and we'd sag together. Then she'd pop up to speak with Marten and come back again later.

What felt like an eternity later, Marten walked over, hands folded behind his back. Baxter slowly straightened. I moved to stand, but Marten put a hand on my shoulder and lowered himself next to me.

"Go home," he murmured, a firm arm looped around my shoulders. "Questioning with the Council and the other delegations can begin soon enough in the morning, when you're fresh. Per Scarlett's request, all the delegations will stay for the next week to unravel . . ." he sighed, "everything."

I reached up and squeezed his hand.

"Thank you."

Marten pulled me to my feet and wrapped me in his arms. I stayed there for a long time, swallowing the sobs and hiccups that threatened to erupt.

"Tomorrow," he murmured. "I'll be here in the morning, waiting for you. We'll face the Council and the delegations together while you tell your story. Go," he whispered, his voice thick with emotion, "and be safe, please."

On his command, I turned to go. Surprisingly, Baxter followed. We'd almost made it to the door when a dark body stopped me.

I halted.

Matthias peered at me down a broad nose and terrifying dark gaze. I stared back. Hadn't I promised a moment like this . . . and delivered? The thrill I'd expected to feel never came. Instead, I felt at odds inside.

Matthias swallowed, his throat working. Then he reached out a forearm.

"I remember," he murmured. "Thank you."

I looked at his arm, then him. With a nod, I accepted the gesture. His warm hand gripped my forearm in his until I broke it off. After another long gaze at Baxter, Matthias turned away. I let out a long, long breath.

Baxter nudged me into the hall.

* * *

Without saying a word, Baxter and I transported to my cottage, but we couldn't get inside.

Trees ringed the outside, their trunks so close they pressed on each other. Where any gap existed, branches had grown. They encompassed Goat's pen in the back in their protection as well. Her plaintive bleats broke the still morning air.

Tears filled my eyes.

I crouched down. My fingers burrowed through a skein of snow and into the ground. The tips dug down even as roots reached up, tangling their delicate strands around my first knuckle. On instinct, I opened my mind to the trees.

She always comes back.

She returns.

You belong to us.

"Always," I whispered, tremulous. The world might quiver. Papa may disappear. Demigods might come. But Letum Wood would never leave me.

Slowly, the trees began to shift away from my home. Roots wound through the forest, burrowing ahead, pulling the trunks farther apart and back into the forest. Gaps appeared. Branches rose. The trees shuffled out just far enough to give us light and space, but no farther. I watched it happen in awe, like the sunset that never grows old.

Once we passed through, the trees settled with soft soughs, still a protective barrier. I trailed my fingers along their rough bark.

"Thank you," I whispered.

Overhead, they sang.

My sentinels.

Once inside, I slipped out of my boots, issuing a spell to the fireplace. Broken plates, an overturned chair, a cracked window. Someone had rampaged my cottage after we left. We wordlessly set everything right while the room warmed from the fire. My thoughts wandered to Papa, then Priscilla, Scarlett, the castle, the city. All over Alkarra, things had been threatened. Burned.

But not destroyed.

A heavy hand on my shoulder drew me out of those deepening thoughts. I blinked, tilting my head back. Baxter jerked his chin toward the bed.

"C'mon. You need sleep."

"You look worse than me," I quipped in a pitiful attempt to restore some normalcy between us.

Something lay there. Something heavy and burdened and uncertain on all sides. A grin split his lips, then he winced, wetting the offended bottom lip with his tongue and a grimace.

"We're both in bad shape," he said, his voice a low, weary roll. "We need to sleep. We both have a lot to answer for tomorrow."

I put a hand over his. "Stay?" I whispered.

He nodded.

Wordless, I turned to my bed. A note lay on my pillow.

With trembling hands, I picked it up and unfolded it with my index finger and thumb. Papa's scratchy handwriting filled the inside.

It was necessary for the good of the Network. I will find you when I'm ready. I'm safe. Please, keep yourself that way.

—Papa

Tears clouded my eyes, blurring the image. I crumbled the note in my hand and lay down. Baxter slid my mat near the fireplace closer to the bed and settled on the floor next to me.

I fell into a fast, dark, swift sleep.

Chapter Twenty-Four

The empty High Priest's apartment sealed off a portion of my life.

How many *merry parts* had I already bid to places and witches that I loved? Too many. This closing door, however, felt more bittersweet than most.

Memories of my time with Papa lived here, still vibrant in the air. If I listened hard enough, I thought I could hear his bright laugh. The clash of our swords as we practiced.

Some of the memories that raced around this place were difficult, harrowing. Others were warm and kind and filled with grace. To say goodbye? It created an ending I hadn't asked for, but still understood.

Marten's unexpected voice echoed around the bare room.

"I've had no word from him."

My voice was an edgy rasp. "You may not," I said without turning around, "until he's ready."

Marten advanced into the room, hands folded behind him.

"It's his right after all he's been through. Losing his birth parents because of his heritage. Serving as a Protector for decades, giving up a normal life with his beloved wife and daughter. Raising you from afar. Becoming High Priest. Losing his mother all over again, fighting a war, destroying Almorran magic, and now a hostile Council that betrayed him."

The heaviness in my chest assigned to Papa leaving without saying goodbye didn't lighten under Marten's review.

The Network may still be reeling from his decision, but soon it would settle. The reports in the *Chatham Chatterer* would slow. Witches would stop speculating about where he had gone and when he would return. Rumors that he'd died and the Council didn't want anyone to know spread like wildfire, then extinguished as quickly. Scarlett had already smoothed out ripples that Papa had never been able to negotiate with the Council, and it all felt like taking a political, fresh breath.

Except I wasn't sure where that left me. Somehow, I couldn't brush Papa's need to run away off like everyone else.

He'd *left* me.

Marten stood at my side. Together, we peered out over the balcony, onto Letum Wood. Despite the ground being several stories below, Letum Wood was still taller than the castle, particularly in the deeper sections of the forest. The smaller growth grew nearer here, the taller in the back.

Would I ever stand on this balcony or in these rooms again?

Unlikely.

Marten's warm hand came to my shoulder as he asked, "How are you?"

"I feel . . . odd."

"The magicks, you mean?"

"Everything. The god magic. The demigod uprising. Papa gone."

"I hope that it goes without saying," he murmured, "that

while your father collects himself back together from all he's been through, I will be here for you. You are mine, Bianca, and cannot escape me so easily."

A smile slipped across my face with his wry, but quite serious, tone. I turned to face him. "Thank you, grandfather."

Stunned, he blinked once. Then twice. His eyes misted.

"Grandfather," he whispered.

"Grandfather."

He swallowed, smiled, and gently shook my shoulder in an affectionate gesture. I embraced him, and he held me tighter than he ever had before.

The familiar staccato of steps leading over to the breakfast nook drew me away. I looked as Reeves approached. His usually droll expression appeared reddened, even strangled. He stopped a few paces away.

"Reeves," I said with amusement, and some sadness. "What will you do now that you don't have to track me down constantly?"

"Gratefully serve the next High Priest," he replied.

I smiled, my lips twitching. "As you always have. You were his most faithful witch and we both love you."

His stolid gaze softened, then looked damp at the edges. He drew in a deep breath, bowed at the waist, and said with a cracking voice, "You will be most missed, Miss Bianca."

"You as well, Reeves."

Emotion thickened my throat. Before he could back away, I threw my arms around him. He staggered back, stiff as a board, and finally put a warm hand on my shoulder to pat it affectionately.

"You are welcome at my post anytime," he said quietly. "Any time."

"Thank you."

Reeves backed away, a sniffle bearing him into the other room. In a week or two, the new High Priest would fill this apartment with his own style. The weapons we left laying around would probably be replaced with parchment. More diplomacy. The intense, sometimes frustrated air that Papa paced around with would settle into thoughtful discussions or late night meetings.

Whatever this apartment became, it would be what the Network needed it to be. And that gave me the greatest comfort of all.

I turned to Marten. "I have a few things to fix at my place," I said quietly. "Would you be up to helping?"

His smile stretched wide. "A grandfather's dream."

* * *

A hooded figure stood in the forest, peering out the opposite direction as I walked up. The broad shoulders, long arms, thick leather boots, were a dead giveaway.

I stepped next to Merrick and looked out at the woods.

"I thought I'd find you here," I said.

"You've rubbed off on me," he murmured. "I find myself drawn to the forest these days. Especially on the hard days."

"It's the forest, not me. It has its own magic unbound by known spells or grimoires. It calls its witches to it."

He let out a long, long breath, as if he'd been holding it this whole time and my presence allowed him to finally release. With the Council and delegation interrogation behind me, where Marten stood firm at my side the whole time, I felt blessedly numb. The ache of missing my father, wishing I had him to speak with, filled me up inside.

Out of sheer willpower, I swallowed it back.

"How are you?" I asked.

"My Council has asked me to return to do a full accounting with them of the actions I took to track down

Jote. They have, apparently, their own questions. Though they gave me the assignment, they want the story."

Merrick had been interviewed by the Central Network Council as well, though not as intensely as me. I had entered the meeting hall as Merrick had left. He'd sent me a bolstering look but appeared tired himself. Bitterness lined his tone now, leading me to believe that it hadn't gone well.

"Has the North spoken with Jote?"

"Yes, before his execution. He responded to truth potions just like Bram. They got the full story out."

"Did it vindicate you?"

He snorted. "Yes, it did."

"Ah. Your Council is still a problem then?" I asked.

"My High Priestess," he muttered.

Geralyn.

Geralyn gave Merrick problems? That startled me. Historically, he'd held a good relationship with Geralyn. What would have changed that now that he'd proven the murder of their former High Priestess?

More details would be pertinent later, when Merrick had a chance to sort all of that out for himself.

For now, I had other matters to put to rest.

"I'm going to Alaysia."

His head snapped to the side, gaze instantly on mine. "What?"

The low-spoken word sent a shiver through me. I kept my gaze straight ahead, determined to see this conversation all the way to its end.

"I must. Papa always said that the best strategy is to hunt while the enemy is down. They're smarting and not sure what happened. There's a lull that I need to take advantage of. I'm the only one that can."

He looked away, cursing under his breath. A pause swelled between us.

"Baxter already said he'd go with me," I said in a rush. "I just . . . I need to at least get an idea of what's really over there. I'm the only one for whom it makes sense."

"It makes *no* sense for anyone," he snapped. "Particularly you. Of highest priority is the fact that several Networks will execute four demigods. Bram. Jote. The one in the East, and the other one. You think the gods won't be angry about that?"

"It does make sense," I said quietly. My hands flexed at my sides. "I'm an amulet of god magic, Merrick. I don't know what that means. The implications need to be figured out. If there's a chance I can get it removed by speaking with Ignis, then I will. At least," I murmured, "I think I will. I carry a part of Ignis in my body. He's part of me. You can't tell me that's a good thing."

His breath was hot and fast, fists clenched at his sides.

"Is this about the Sisterhood?"

"No."

"You don't have to prove yourself anymore, B. This is madness. I can't . . ."

He stalled, at a loss. The muscles in his jaw worked as he struggled with what to say next.

"Can't what?" I asked quietly.

"Can't protect you there."

Anguish filled his voice. I finally met his gaze, not surprised to find the heady emotion mirrored there. A knot formed in my throat, forcing me to swallow past it.

"Maybe you're not supposed to always protect me," I whispered. "Maybe we're supposed to protect Alkarra together."

He studied me, then looked away. A thousand unsaid things lay between us, but I wasn't sure where to start. As if our relationship was an unraveling tapestry, and I couldn't find the threads to tie it back together.

"Is this about you and Baxter?" he asked, throat working. "Is—"

"No."

My immediate rebuttal didn't seem to calm him. How did I fill the quiet after that? Merrick and I had made no promises to each other. He had unfinished business in the North, and I in Alaysia. Both of us had witches we wanted to protect, and no possibility of making any guarantees to anyone.

A lull existed where love had once been—at least on my part. I didn't know what to do with all the emotional tension and baggage still between us.

"I'll be back," I said firmly. "As soon as I can. I need to get the god magic out of me and stop the demigods for good. We've put a little bandage over a big wound. I have little hope that Prana will be satisfied, even if we did stop the first uprising."

Finally, he nodded. It was a weak version of a capitulation.

"I understand," he murmured.

"Do you?"

The question came out of me unbidden, but I didn't regret it. He hesitated, then nodded. His gaze drifted back to mine, filled with walls and uncertainty and a sense, however minor, of resolve.

"I'll be here when you get back," he said firmly. "Waiting. And if there's a way for me to get over there and help you, consider it done."

"Thank you," I whispered.

The forest remained still around us.

Chapter Twenty-Five

Letum Wood breathed around me with a wintry
stillness. Snow drifted gracefully in erratic, fat flakes,
stopped from their falling path by the numerous
branches overhead. By the time they reached the ground,
they'd have gathered on several limbs and fallen in long,
chasing drapes.

I closed my eyes, breathed in the silence.

She has returned.

You belong to us.

She approves.

You will preserve us.

A voice pulled me from their words. "Leda and Hiddleston tell me that you are goddess-touched."

Scarlett stepped up next to me. Together we studied the
forest. Out of the corner of my eye, I could see Scarlett's
concentration. The weight of the world she willingly took on
her own shoulders.

Scarlett could be the right solution for a problem Alkarra
had never, in written history, dealt with before. She had a

diplomatic background Papa didn't. Her attention to relationships, details, and bargaining would smooth over the edges that Papa's life experiences didn't allow him to do. Not in this climate.

That didn't make it easy for her.

We were by no means out of danger. If anything, we hovered just on the edge, ready to plunge into the chasm. But we hadn't fallen yet.

Scarlett remained quiet for a long time, then turned to me. I faced her, feeling just like that lost little girl she'd first met at Miss Mabel's School for Girls.

"You did the right thing, Bianca. The brave thing. You and Leda saved your Network last week, and I want to thank you for it."

I nodded.

Her gaze softened and she became less the Highest Witch and more my friend. Her hand reached up to touch my arm, just above my elbow.

"Your father insisted on giving me the Highest Witch power early, just to make it easier on me. He thought he had a good chance of dying when the demigods broke into the castle, but he had planned on relinquishing the title for months. I didn't see the wisdom in it, not until now, but he was right. The Network would never have had peace under this Council with him in power." She smiled. "Of course, trust your father to break all convention and set a new precedent for history—all on his own terms, of course."

I managed a trying smile. "Papa was always good at that."

Scarlett sobered. "Now, we have a real mess to face. If I'm going to carry us through this, it will be because of my unprecedented love for big goals. A Sisterhood will be more important than ever."

"You always have it," I promised.

She nodded.

"How does it feel?" I asked quietly, a mirror of the same question I'd asked Papa on the day he became Highest Witch. Her gaze became distant for a moment. When she blinked it away with a light shake of her head, she looked weary. Unlike Papa, however, a bright current of energy and determination ran through her, shucking aside the restless frustration he'd always felt.

Scarlett was *ready*.

"Strange," she murmured. "Like the weight of the world rests on my shoulders, but I know it doesn't. My magic is quicker and stronger. It responds sooner to my commands and with more power. Something in becoming Highest Witch, through the Esmelda scrolls, has given me greater ability. It's . . . helpful."

"You were made for this, Scarlett."

She eyed me. "So were you."

A smile found me again. There were new hollows in my heart. Empty places that reverberated with the sounds of what had been, what I wanted to be. Ways I'd shifted, grown, changed. But new things had come to replace the old ones. Unknown strength. A different ferocity. Determination. Willing patience. It had all become a part of me.

I drew in a deep breath.

"The Sisterhood has two members," I murmured. "Me, Leda, and . . . Ava, though she's still on probation and doesn't count. I couldn't deny her," I added, chuckling. "She's insistent, you know?"

Scarlett's lips twitched. "Just like your father. Breaking precedent and history on your own terms."

"All of us are committed to serving *you*, Scarlett. We're unlikely to get assignments from Council Members, but we might from you. Know that we're ready. For whatever you wish. Though I must ask—what about Bram? What have you decided?"

"He has already been executed on my orders."

My eyes grew wide. "When?"

"This morning. I watched him die myself. A macabre duty for the Highest Witch, but oddly appropriate, if you ask me."

Stunned, I could only stare at her. Although regret stained her tone, it was overpowered by the sense of confidence that only Scarlett could portray.

"He'd betrayed us twice," she said. "Attempted a rebellious takeover. There was no need for another chance."

"The Council approved, I hope?" I murmured.

"Wholeheartedly."

After a moment I whispered, "Me too."

A fleeting amusement passed over her face, then faded. "Thank you, I think. Regardless, his effects were left behind. In fact, I thought they might be of interest to you. I brought them with me."

She reached into her pocket, pulling out a small box the size of her palm. Wooden, but without a discernible opening. All lines in the box were smooth, unblemished, and gleaned. Words scripted on the outside in a language I didn't recognize.

"Puzzle box?" I murmured.

"Pressure on the top, bottom, and lower left should do it."

My fingers squeezed the areas she indicated and one of the edges slid open, I pulled it the rest of the way. Inside lay Bram's amulet. I studied it, then looked at her silently.

Scarlett took a step back.

"The Central Network," she said in her High Priestess voice, "cannot condone the actions you took a week ago without complicit approval. Some have been calling it insubordination, but those complaints have been subdued out of gratitude that all worked to our advantage in the end. We can't have witches springing up as vigilantes, taking justice in hand on their own."

Something cold slipped through me, but her queer, intent gaze kept me from abandoning all hope. With a touch from my hand, the puzzle box slid shut. I pushed it into my dress pocket, watching her carefully.

Scarlett stepped back again.

"The Sisterhood is not a recognized, supported protective force in the Central Network at this time. I cannot condone you, a goddess-touched witch that also holds the magic of the gods, going to Alaysia to assess the situation surrounding the gods. Even if Baxter has agreed to go with you as escort and aid, with Ava at his side, this is not an act that the High Priestess would sanction without Council approval."

Understanding flooded me.

Oh.

A tingle preceded the realization. She knew my plans already. Or had guessed at them, at any rate, and sought to approve.

In her own diplomatic, preserve-the-Council's-pride sort of way.

The way Papa would never have cared about.

Scarlett folded her hands in front of her and motioned with a little nod of her head toward my pocket where the amulet lay.

"The Council is aware that, in the chaos that followed Bram's attempted uprising in the High Priest's office, the amulet he used was lost." She gave a little frown. "The Council is very upset, and Halifax is seeking an official inquiry into the matter. It was an unfortunate mistake on our part, but one that was understandable considering the circumstances. We regret that it happened."

I licked my lips. "Understood."

Scarlett nodded. She'd fully returned back to the Highest Witch I knew so well. Remnants of the Network school teacher still hummed in her, making it obvious that she'd transitioned back to who she now needed to be.

"Due to recent activities," she continued, "I think it would be wise for you if some time were spent away from the Central Network. Wherever and whatever you decide is on you. Please, be cautious on your . . . adventure. You are the daughter of the great Derek Black, Bianca, and bright is your future. I would like to be part of it. Not to forget your best friend and compatriot, who would be *very* upset not to join you on said mission. I truly forbid that, for I cannot do this without her."

My fingers closed around the box as I nodded. Wind whistled past me, sending my hair off my shoulders in weak banners. We watched each other, swamped with a mutual feeling of despair, love, and hope for the future. I wanted to hug her, but sensed both of us might break.

"Thank you, Scarlett. Anytime you want to let your hair down . . ."

A suppressed grin twitched her lips. "Be safe, my friend," she whispered.

And Scarlett was gone.

The trees murmured around me, their voices slipping through my mind with their usual soothing, calming presence. A burst of blue light near the closest tree drew my attention. I put my hand on Viveet's hilt and stepped closer.

Words appeared on the trunk in a bright, scripted handwriting. The color matched Viveet almost exactly. I moved in closer, peering at it.

Prepare yourself.

The words faded away, as if leaking back into the tree. I ran my fingers over the bark, the ominous promise rippling through my mind. Then I stepped away, my hand ghosting down the tree.

I had a trip to plan.

373

THE END

Note from the Author

I hope you absolutely loved RISE OF THE DEMIGODS and the next step in Bianca's grand adventures.

While you're here, would you do me a favor? I'd love it if you dropped a review of RISE OF THE DEMIGODS on my website.

Just visit www.katiecrossbooks.com and type the title into the search bar. The paperback version will pop right up.

Other readers love to hear what you think—it helps them know they've found the right book. Putting it on my site means we know it won't get deleted—no matter the rating!

(Some retailers will delete sincere, honest readers review at their own discretion and without explanation. That sort of censoring is ridiculous, so we like to give you a spot to *know* your review is safe!)

Thanks in advance!

—Katie

PS—If you keep reading, you'll get a sneak peek into the next two books in the Network Saga: PRISCILLA and THE FORGOTTEN GODS.

Priscilla

NOVELLA #4 IN THE NETWORK SAGA

The edge of a heavy wooden door caught Priscilla's slip and snagged it. She stumbled, jerked backward by the tug. Her hand shot out and caught the wall before she tumbled feet-over-head down the back stairway of Magnolia castle.

She closed her eyes, drew in a deep breath, and let it back out.

Calmly, she reminded herself. *I must be calm. Everything is fine. I can't act unusual or frightened.*

Everything. Is. Fine.

With all her determination, she pasted on a smile, freed her dress, and moved forward again. A servant hurried closer, arm outstretched.

"Mistress?" she called.

Priscilla waved a hand, flashed a smile, and darted through the doorway at the top of the stairs. Heat and acid built at the back of her throat, scorching the already raw skin there. She pressed her lips together.

I will not vomit on the floor.

I will not vomit on the floor.

She navigated expertly through the beautiful halls laid

with marble, history, and echoes of blood. The back way moved like second nature. Left there. Right here. Around the circle, take the back stairs to the third floor and . . . there.

A rumbling voice greeted her as she turned into Niko's sprawling suites on the third floor.

"Miss Priscilla, are you well?"

The voice belonged to Gaston, an East Guard assigned to Niko's quarters, and one of her most loyal friends. His broad forehead furrowed into lines, framed by dark hair pulled into a shiny queue at the back of his head. She shook her head, tears in her eyes as she frantically rushed toward him.

"What is wrong?" he called.

With a hand pressed to her mouth, she waved for him to open the door. Understanding flooded his gaze. He twisted the handle and threw it open.

She sailed through, hurried to the back, out the open double doors, and vomited over the side porch.

After retching two times, emptying what little she'd nibbled on during the picnic with Bianca, her legs collapsed beneath her. Limp as a noodle, she slid bonelessly to the stone floor and pressed her face to the cool, smooth ground.

The tempest in her stomach calmed. Her banging head eased slightly. All that had rocked and churned in her body for the last half hour now settled like a baby about to sleep. Priscilla closed her eyes and sighed.

Better.

Gaston's inquiring, concerned tone followed. He stood in the doorway, one hand on the hilt of his sword.

"Miss Priscilla?"

The cold floor on her flushed cheeks anchored her into the day again. She used a sweaty hand to wipe the hair off her face.

"I'm fine," she whispered in Ilese. "I'm fine. Thank you, Gaston."

"Shall I call for an apothecary?"

Priscilla jerked upright. "No!"

Gaston's eyes widened. He shuffled back a step. She passed a weary hand over her eyes. In a softer tone she said, "I'm sorry, Gaston. It's a passing problem, that's all. A mild flu. No need to draw any attention to it."

"I'll call for Marguerite."

"Please, no." She pushed herself to a sitting position. Her stomach bobbled for a moment, but it quickly subsided. "Truly, Gaston, I'm fine. Marguerite is on her lunch break. Allow her at least that much time to herself. She works too hard for me as it is."

"She would not like—"

"If you could just get me some water to rinse my mouth, I'd be grateful. I'll remain calm and quiet until she returns. It will be soon enough. There's nothing she would do that we can't figure out together."

His eyebrows crashed together. Clearly, he didn't like it. He left, then returned with a glass of water. His thick fingers were gentle when he handed it over, bright brown eyes still wary.

"You're pale."

Priscilla sipped the water, swished it around, then spat it back out. It crashed somewhere below, and she suppressed a groan at the thought that someone might have already seen her vomit.

Like always, he somehow read her mind. "Marguerite will take care of it," he murmured. He crouched next to her now, his sword jutting out at an odd angle near his left hip.

She smiled softly. "Thank you, Gaston. I just sent a spell to clean it up. It's not her job."

"She is your maid!"

"My friend," Priscilla said gently. She put a clammy hand on his wrist. "As are you. You are more to me than castle servants."

He chortled, and it sounded like a bass in his barrel chest.

"Then allow me to inform someone else next time and have *them* clean it up. It's not for the future High Priestess to worry about."

His words echoed in her mind.

Future High Priestess.

Is that what I am? she thought. She secretly carried the High Priest's baby, wore his cord of engagement every day, and lived in his personal quarters for the last two years. By all accounts, she should be the love of his life.

But a witch *handfasted* the love of his life.

He didn't string her along with empty promises and platitudes, exacting what he needed, but incapable of returning it. She mentally shook herself. Was that a fair attitude to have toward Niko? He faced an exorbitant amount of pressure from his own Council these days. He was a High Priest.

What High Priest had time for a handfasting?

Priscilla swilled the water around the cup, watching it spin. History dictated that thousands of former High Priests had time for a handfasting and a family besides. Not Niko, though.

And now?

Now there was a mortal loose in Alkarra. No, not loose. The girl was with Bianca. Perhaps the best—or worst—witch to have found her. Bianca would keep the girl safe, but was that the most important thing?

Who would keep Bianca safe?

A chill slipped down Priscilla's arms.

If Bianca hadn't saved the mortal girl, the Eastern Network Council would have eventually put her to death. Likely, they would have used her as a pawn, a political up-level at the Celebration. Niko might have squeezed the girl to his advantage against the Central Network.

Wasn't it his right?

No. Not with a child's life at stake.

Saving the girl from the East meant more than just sparing her life. It had drawn a firm line in the metaphorical sand. Apparently Priscilla's heart still belonged to the Central Network, for she feared what the East would do against them. The Central Network, after all, held the title of *home*.

At least, it used to be home.

Her parents didn't speak to her. They wouldn't. Not until there was a handfasting to *make right what you've done by living in the same apartment as him for two years*. None of the girls she attended school with except Bianca, Leda, and Michelle spoke with her. She'd let go of the other witches from school with only a little sadness. Moving to the Eastern Network had been as easy as breathing.

These days?

She craved safety. Someone to care for her.

Gaston's voice drew Priscilla back out of her thoughts.

"Are you sure you're well? You don't . . . you don't seem like yourself. Did something happen at your luncheon?"

She smiled to reassure him, then held out a hand. He helped to pull her to her feet. She wouldn't have asked for the help, but knew he'd give it anyway. Being useful brought him joy.

"I assure you," she murmured, "I feel much better already. I'll sit out here in the fresh air and the cool breeze until Marguerite returns. The ocean always restores me."

He brightened. "A nap, perhaps? Sleep fixes everything."

"Yes."

With one last, lingering look, Gaston returned inside. After a quick scan of the room, he ducked his head in each closet and adjoining area, cleared the apartment of possible threats, and stepped back out into the hall.

Priscilla lowered herself into a padded wicker chair, closed her eyes, leaned her head back, and let the ocean air cool her fevered skin.

The panic of the mortal girl, the fear of Magnolia castle staff seeing her vomit, faded. If just one witch here suspected that she was with child, her house of cards would topple.

Her body relaxed into the seat cushions, and sleep washed in like the tide. Her mind drifted back to the early days with Niko. The desperate days when the Network recovered from war, Niko formed his own authority with the Council, and she had been indispensable at his side.

They'd worked together then, yet she rarely saw him now. The male witch Mordecai had moved into the castle as a *special consultant* to Niko over a year ago.

Really, he'd almost overtaken Hector's place as Assistant, except Hector was too bulldog-stubborn to let Mordecai edge him out entirely.

When Mordecai had shown up, Priscilla's importance began to fade. Niko needed her less, set her aside more often. Their conversations became as brittle as dried seaweed and tempestuous as the stormy winter skies. Questions about what had gone wrong, why he acted so quiet, plagued her eternally.

Mordecai, she thought bitterly.

Niko didn't even see it.

She needed to leave. To create a safe home for her child away from Niko and his significant power here. No later than tomorrow, in fact.

Now that Bianca had offered her cottage, Priscilla could walk away. Didn't even need to pack. The only tie to the East lay in blood and bones.

Her baby.

Her love.

Somehow, she'd start a new life without Niko and everyone she loved in the East. A life that would be safe for her child. In the end, she didn't know if the Eastern Network

Council would do something drastic to an Aldana baby born out of handfasting. They might ignore her, but that seemed unlikely.

Would Niko abandon them?

Would she and the baby survive?

She didn't know.

She slipped into sleep with the thought that the answers didn't matter anymore. With Bianca's help, she would start her brand new life.

If you're reading to read more about Priscilla and Niko's story in The Network Saga, **visit www.katiecrossbooks.com** to buy your paperback version today.

(It's not available for purchase on the retailers.)

The Forgotten Gods

A SNEAK PEEK INTO THE NETWORK
SAGA BOOK #3

Goat bleated unhappily in her pen.

I stood inside my cottage and regarded the wintry day with a shiver. Sometime in the night, the youngest saplings had rearranged themselves. They all stood closer to my cottage now, but not so close that I couldn't see beyond them.

Enough that I noticed.

But why?

In the back of my mind, the trees continued to croon softly. Their anxiety had risen overnight, as if they knew what I was about to do.

A moment later, a rap came on my door. With it came a flash of familiar, friendly heat in my blood, like someone had dumped warm water in my veins. I opened the door with a spell and a twist of my stomach.

Baxter stepped inside, Ava at his side. Both of them lacked their usual levity and brightness. A solemn shroud draped them.

Ava wore her hair down around her shoulders, the black and reddish strands loose to her elbows now. Her eyes were solemn, her expression drawn, as if she hadn't slept well last night.

Next to her, Baxter didn't look much better. Bags lay under his eyes, a testament to the hellish week that had passed since the rise of the demigods, and subsequent fall. Papa had disappeared, Scarlett had taken over as Highest Witch, and that left a lot of questions in the meantime. Not to mention chaos in the Network, upset Council Members for various reasons, and more.

Now, we had bigger enemies to face.

Baxter cleared his throat and asked with a gentle rasp, "Are you ready?"

"You look anything but excited," I murmured.

My hope for some enthusiasm died. All of us sounded like a funeral dirge. Baxter and Ava knew what to expect in returning to Alaysia, but I did not. A bleak start that I was the only one with some sort of eagerness over the trip.

New lands.

Different magic.

Wild places.

"There's nothing exciting about returning to Alaysia," Baxter murmured, "except for the hope to remove god magic from you, of course, and break any connection you have with Ignis."

A second shiver traveled all the way up my spine. Ignis, god of fire. Somehow I'd managed not only to get his magic trapped inside my body, but to become an amulet of god magic myself. A connection existed between me and the god of fire—the last week had proven that.

But *what* that connection meant still hadn't been decided. An ominous thing considering how many of his demigod children had now died in Alkarra, and how many amulets he lost to witches now.

Most of which happened at my own hand.

"It will be worth it," I said.

Baxter nodded. "I hope so. I don't know what to expect from Ignis. I don't know if he'll see you or remove the magic or just kill you right away. Are you sure it's a chance you want to take?"

"Yes."

His lips pressed into a thin, annoyed line. There was more to our Alaysian trip than just removing my magic. It was my chance to get more information. To see what Alkarrans faced. Questions abounded now more than ever.

How many demigods? Could I speak with the gods? Unlikely, for the latter, too many for the former.

Still, I had to know.

Only a witch could go there and get the information we needed. Did goddess magic work in the land of the gods? If not, why? If so, was it the same? Did spells and incantations cross the distance? Could I transport a message back to Leda?

These questions and more hung on me, almost as heavy as our nearly-non-existent plan.

How we would get Ignis to remove my magic, then return me safely here, was all left to chance. Baxter's ability to magick us to and from Alaysia was our only hope of returning.

Whatever came next, I anticipated brimstone, fire, and darkness. A land filled with miserable mortals, too many demigods roaming around in a search for power, and bitterness at every landscape.

The real Alaysia couldn't be worse than what I imagined in my head.

"Shall we get this over with?" I asked. "The sooner we can talk to Ignis and your father, the sooner we can come back. With any luck, this will take one day, maybe two."

Baxter frowned, his face clouded, but he only nodded.

Ava reached for my hand. With a smile, I accepted. Her small fingers against mine felt warm.

"I'm taking us to my father's house first," Baxter murmured. "There, we'll get settled. Then my sisters and I will take you on a tour. Tonight, I will be able to get more information from my father about whether he wants to meet you, or if he can help us convince Ignis to free your magic."

I nodded.

"A good start."

His lacking enthusiasm didn't give me much hope, but I ignored it. Ava shuffled closer to my side, so I dropped an arm on her shoulder. Her solid warmth gave me some comfort, and I hoped I did the same for her.

The fire in my body brightened as I held my hand out to Baxter, as if the god magic knew something was about to happen. Baxter looked at my fingers, then my eyes, then seemed to steel himself.

With grim resolve he threaded his fingers through mine.

My cottage disappeared.

* * *

We arrived at the land of the gods within a blink.

Warmth welcomed me first. Gentle. Beguiling. Like the perfect, mild day before the ferocity of summer. Sand welled up between my toes, warm and soft. The smell of sea foam lingered in the air.

When I opened my eyes, brilliant sunshine blinded me. I held up an arm, Baxter's fingers untangling from mine. A gentle breeze whispered by, playing with strands of my hair. I gazed out on a bright ocean, stretching all the way to the horizon in front of me.

Did Alkarra lay on the other side?

I sucked in a sharp breath and turned around. A white sand beach crawled behind us, heading toward a sprawling structure made out of sand and small, green trees. The beach swept upward in a daunting castle of sand. Turrets and baileys and space filled the area, twice the width of Chatham Castle though half as tall.

"The good gods," I murmured.

Two women walked toward us from the daunting structure, smiling. Baxter braced himself. Ava sucked in a sharp breath, then growled. Her fingers tightened on me as she stepped in front of me.

Baxter followed suit.

My breath came fast as reality settled in my mind. I had come to Alaysia, the land of the gods, and it was nothing like what I'd expected.

A familiar, quiet voice whispered through my mind.

Welcome, witch, Ignis murmured softly, like a low candle at night. *Welcome to the land of the gods.*

I look forward to meeting you.

If you haven't purchased your copy of THE FORGOTTEN GODS yet, then grab it **at www.katiecrossbooks.com** or any online book retailer.

So you don't miss any of the adventure :)

Join Other Witches

Merry meet!

There is more epic magic and wild places waiting for you.

If you want to stay in-the-know about new releases, get awesome discounts (IE—more books, less money), and have free novels and short stories land in your lap, I've got your back.

Go to www.katiecrossbooks.com to join the other witches on my email list, where you get exclusive, can't-find-anywhere-else kind of stuff.

(In fact, I'll send you some free stories right away—first email!)

Or you can go to The Witchery, which is my Facebook group of other readers just like you. Just visit www.facebook.com/groups/thenetworkseries.

There, you'll see more images of Alkarra, join all your witchy friends, and go to lunch with me on my weekly Coffee With Katie calls.

(No, seriously. I will Uber-Eats you lunch!)

Can't wait to see you there!

—Katie

Acknowledgments

Wow, where do I even start?

First, my team. Samantha, Kristen, Mike, Jesse, Darcee, Gemma, Evan, Kaley, Brandy, and Jenn-ay. What would these books be without you to help me push them into the world?

Lame, that's what!

Thank you for all you do. For the support, the love, the coworking calls, the rampant honesty, and the laughs. I sent you so many messages asking for help and critique and answers and affirmation that I had done the right thing. THANK YOU.

Kelsey Keating, this ENTIRE SAGA would never have unfolded without our late night, hours-long calls. My creativity is activated by your brain and together, we are powerful.

My family—you put up with a lot. Space-out sessions, recording voice messages to myself while I'm driving and think of an idea, and late nights listening to music when I tune the world out and just write.

I adore and love you all.

To my readers, I hope you love this continuation of Bianca's story as much as me. To push her farther into the world, to find our courage and adventures, is my life joy. The only greater thing for my book is the emails and messages I receive as you enjoy living in her shoes.

For all you do, thank you.

Hazel (short story)

The Network Saga Suggested Reading Order

1. The Parting (novella #1)

2. The Lost Magic (full-length novel)

3. The Lamplighter's Daughter (novella #2)

4. Merrick (novella #3)

5. The Rise of the Demigods (full-length novel)

6. Priscilla (novella #4)

7. Viveet (novella #5)

8. Prana (novella #6)

9. Derek (novella #7)

10. The Forgotten Gods (full-length novel)

11. The Returning (novella #8)

12. Regina (novella #9)

13. Leda (novella #10)

14. The Sister (prequel to WOTG #1)

15. The School (prequel to WOTG #2)

16. The Council (prequel to WOTG #3)

17. The Goddess (prequel to WOTG #4)

18. War of the Gods (full-length novel)

19. The Finales (a collection of novellas)

20. Marten (novella #11)

The Historical Collection

The High Priestess

The Swordmaker

The Advocate

The Reader Request Series

The Gods

The Plummet

The North

The Wander

The Return

Viveet Forged

About the Author

Katie Cross is ALL ABOUT writing epic magic and wild places. Creating new fantasy worlds is her jam.

When she's not hiking or chasing her two littles through the Montana mountains, you can find her curled up reading a book or arguing with her husband over the best kind of sushi.

Visit her at www.katiecrossbooks.com for free short stories, extra savings on all her books (and some you can't buy on the retailers), and so much more.